ERNESTO GA

THE HORRIBLE DR. HICHCOCK

THE NOVEL

MICHAEL HUDSON

*BASED ON THE ORIGINAL SCREENPLAY
BY ERNESTO GASTALDI*

NEVER SAY NEVERMORE

First Edition • June 2015 • Editing, arrangement and presentation of the material is copyright © 2015 Ernesto Gastaldi and Michael Hudson, Raven's Head Press. All rights reserved.

Foreword © 2015 by Dave Brzeski. All rights reserved.

Book Designer: Michael Hudson

Book Editor: Christi Clore

The Leper by Algernon Charles Swinburne: Poems and Ballads 1866

PUBLISHERS NOTE

This novel was translated and adapted directly from Ernesto Gastaldi's original screenplay of *"L'ORRIBILE SEGRETO DEL DR. HITCHCOK"*. We hope you, the reader, will enjoy the variances from the filmed version.

Except for brief passages used in reviews or critical articles, no part of this publication may be reproduced, stored in or introduced into a retrieval system, or transmitted, in any form or by any means (electronic, mechanical, photocopying, or otherwise) without the prior written permission of Raven's Head Press.
ISBN-13: 978-0692467282 • ISBN-10: 0692467289

TO

GIANLUCA PIREDDIA

Foreword

There are several ways to go about writing a movie novelization. The author can choose to expand on, or clarify events that the film leaves too vague—even add entirely new scenes to fill perceived gaps in the narrative. The publisher, as in the recent run of Hammer film novelizations, may decide it would be more commercial to update the stories to a more modern setting. While I've enjoyed many such books, I often really wish they'd just be faithful to the original work and this is exactly what Michael Hudson has striven for here.

The source in this case, is the original screenplay, as written by Ernesto Gastaldi, so the reader will find some small differences between this book and the final film. This does actually serve to clarify aspects of the story that were left necessarily somewhat vague in the film, due to what would be considered acceptable by the censors of the time. It's regarding this clarification issue that the author has been remarkably clever. It would have been so easy to simply describe certain scenes in a much more explicit manner. However, Michael Hudson manages to make it perfectly clear what is going on without adding anything that wasn't actually in the script. Every scene in this book was in the movie, or would have been if they'd stayed absolutely true to the script.

I suppose, if you were to try to describe the story, you'd have to say it falls into the mad scientist sub-genre. It's far more complex than that, though. The good Doctor Hichcock is not performing experiments that would horrify the scientific establishment, like a Frankenstein. In his professional life, he's a good and respected surgeon. He's developed a new anaesthetic, which would be a boon to all surgeons, and even more so for their patients.

No, it's the use he puts his newly developed drug to in his personal life that would have him pilloried by anyone who knew about it. The fact that his first wife was happy to go along with him in this would, I have no doubt, give pause to most modern women for any number of reasons. It's never revealed if he ever even approached his second wife about his peculiar needs, but if he did, she was understandably reticent.

Michael Hudson does not judge. He simply presents the facts, as they were in the script and leaves it to the reader to decide if the unfortunate Doctor Hichcock is equally deserving of pity as he is of scorn.

—Dave Brzeski

British Fantasy Society Reviewer

ERNESTO GASTALDI'S
THE HORRIBLE DR. HICHCOCK

THE NOVEL

MICHAEL HUDSON

BASED ON THE ORIGINAL SCREENPLAY BY ERNESTO GASTALDI

CHAPTER ONE

Nothing is better, I well think,
Than love; the hidden well-water
Is not so delicate to drink:
This was well seen of me and her.

I served her in a royal house;
I served her wine and curious meat.
For will to kiss between her brows,
I had no heart to sleep or eat.
           —Algernon Charles Swinburne

LONDON 1885

Highgate Cemetery sat atop a four hundred-foot hill overlooking London. During the day it was a lovely place filled with serpentine paths shaded by a canopy of ancient towering oaks, silver birch, willows, and chestnut trees.

It contained spectacular marble and granite headstones and weathered mausoleums adorned with sculpted figures of angels, gargoyles, and animals of all sorts, some hidden, but many on prominent display among a lush tangle of ivy, moss, and hollyhocks.

The old Western Cemetery wall was surrounded by a high wall and barred with heavy wrought iron gates. The newer Eastern Cemetery wall was much less imposing surrounded by a Tudor style wall of yellow brick with a stone dressing.

A common escape of Victorian society for families and young lovers was to spend Sunday afternoons in the Cemetery having picnics and walking the thirty-seven acres studying the ancient headstones.

But at night, the Cemetery was very different from the day. It was a dark, lonely place. And it was no place for the living. Except for the regular patrol of a few policemen on the Western wall, an occasional ground worker digging a new grave, and, of course, the ubiquitous resurrectionists and grave robbers, it was, indeed, a place of the dead.

The night was dark and blustery. An October chill was in the air that caused branches to sing their eerie melodies and leaves to dance across ground and stone. A thick yellow haze swirled at waist level and dampness pervaded the landscape.

The silhouette of a man with a top hat on his head approached the Eastern Wall, placed a gloved hand on the latch of an iron gate and paused. He cocked his head a bit as the great bell affectionately known by Londoners as Big Ben played Westminster Quarters followed by ten tolls of the massive bell.

He turned his head to the South in the direction of the sound. The man could see the twinkling lights of London below him. The lights represented life. However, he was not seeking life, just the opposite. It was death that the man sought that night.

The gate swung open silently and the man made his way swiftly through the maze of stones and gardens led only by the light of the moon. He soon came upon a little man bent over lost in his work whistling a jaunty tune to accompany his shovel-fulls of dirt that he tossed to the side of a new grave. A polished beech coffin sat behind the gravedigger.

Upon spying the gravedigger, there was no hesitation. The man strode boldly up to him and stabbed him in the back of the neck. The little man's whistle turned into a gargle as he fell into the pit he had been digging.

The man sighed then rubbed his hands together and turned to the coffin. One end contained a small oblong glass window. He rubbed a gloved hand over it to remove the moisture. Behind the glass was the face of a woman. The man shivered and his eyes seemed to dilate as he peered at the face behind the glass.

He bent down and undid the three latches, lifted the lid, and pushed it to the side. The man methodically removed his gloves and blew into his hands as he rubbed them together. He then began to caress the body of the dead woman in a slow, sensual gesture.

The majestic red brick building stood at the corner of Gower Street and Grafton Way in Bloomsbury, Central London. Two gas streetlamps at its entrance revealed large brass letters above the portico that spelled out: UNIVERSITY COLLEGE LONDON.

Several groups of young men stood outside on the steps of the hospital's main entrance, some in their hospital whites and others in topcoat and hat. They smoked and chatted about classes, teachers, and sex.

University College Hospital was a teaching hospital and, as such, almost every surgery performed was observed by a number of students and interns.

The white room was actually a small amphitheater. The walls were roughly nine feet in height and gave way to a 360-degree seating area surrounded by an iron railing that ran around the room.

The seating area was darkened. It was also packed with students. There was no chatting going on here. All eyes were intently focused on the operation soon to be taking place in the room below them.

A large oil lamp threw a yellow glow on the operating table upon which lay the body of a woman partly covered by a white sheet.

A team of surgeons led by Dr. Bernard Hichcock stood around the operating table. Dr. Hichcock commanded the attention of the room not only for his authoritative demeanor and voice but also for his appearance. He was a man of about fifty years of age and he stood just over six feet tall. With his aristocratic looks, dark hair, and knitted eyebrows he presented a rather imposing figure.

Hichcock stood over the body of the woman in a white surgical gown, mask, and white gloves. He observed the woman for a moment and then spoke to her saying, "You will not feel anything. It will be as if you were asleep," and then to one of his assistants, "Nurse, anesthetic, please."

The nurse prepared a syringe and handed it to the doctor. He held it up to the light while giving it a small push to release any air bubbles and then injected the syringe into the arm of the moaning patient.

Looking up into the amphitheater he said, "This anesthetic slows the heart rate; we must operate before her heart rate returns to normal."

Many of the students pulled out their pocket watches to mark the time.

Two of the assistants stepped forward to serve as dressers and held the woman's shoulders. One of them placed a cork gag in between her teeth.

The doctor addressed them, "Stay where you are, but holding the patient should not be necessary."

Hichcock rubbed his hands together then looked down as he began to call for the surgical instruments needed to perform the delicate operation. "Scalpel, suction, clamp..."

An hour later, Dr. Hichcock stood just outside the operating room. He removed his blood-spattered gown and handed it to an assistant. Underneath he wore a well-tailored evening suit.

The assistant helped him with his overcoat and handed him his hat. The younger man seemed perplexed and hesitant but then gathered his courage and asked, "Professor, are you sure that—"

"Not now, Evans! We are having guests for dinner tonight. If I delay, my wife will kill me!"

The young man lowered his eyes and wilted under Hichcock's penetrating glare.

Before Hichcock could turn to leave another assistant turned the corner in a run and called out his name.

"Professor? Ho, Professor?" He screeched to a halt directly in front of the doctor.

Hichcock, obviously aggravated, looked at the young man and said, "Yes, what is it?"

"I'm sorry, Sir, but there's a Commissioner Scott who wants to see you!"

"Tell him I will meet him downstairs in the lobby."

Commissioner Scott stood in the lobby waiting for Dr. Hichcock. He was an older man with a full head of silver hair and a trim mustache to match. He wore a black frock coat, burgundy silk vest, and a dove gray cravat and gloves. He topped this off with a large black cloak lined with silk. He held a dark gray wool derby in his hands.

A nondescript young woman in a dark shawl accompanied him. She sat in a chair sniffling into a proffered handkerchief from the Commissioner.

Commissioner Scott looked down at the young woman with compassion and said, "There, there, child. We'll soon know something. There is no practitioner in London better than Dr. Hichcock!"

He looked up to see Dr. Hichcock approaching at a rapid walk. The doctor was not smiling. The Commissioner addressed him with a friendly greeting, "Bernard, how are you my friend?"

Hichcock replied tersely, "I'm well."

The Commissioner's eyes narrowed, but he did not miss a beat. He went straight to the point and asked, "Do you think she'll pull through?"

"As you well know, Commissioner, it was a bad injury. I did everything I could to save her. I'm sorry, but I am in a hurry. Tomorrow I hope to find our patient out of danger. Good evening."

The Commissioner bowed slightly and replied, "Thank you, Bernard, and good night to you."

Dr. Hichcock had already turned and was walking out of the lobby.

The Commissioner turned back to the young woman who looked up from the handkerchief with expectant eyes. He said, "If the Professor has done everything possible to save her, you can rest easy. You'll see that your sister will soon be well."

CHAPTER TWO

Mere scorn God knows she had of me,
A poor scribe, nowise great or fair,
Who plucked his clerk's hood back to see
Her curled-up lips and amorous hair.

I vex my head with thinking this.
Yea, though God always hated me,
And hates me now that I can kiss
Her eyes, plait up her hair to see.

Rubens House was a beautiful red brick mansion that sat facing the famed gardens in Mecklenburgh Square just a few miles northeast of University Hospital. Of English Victorian design, the impressive great house had lovely terraces decorated with geometric patterns that looked out over a large expanse of lawn filled with sculpted gardens and mature trees.

A variegated wrought iron fence surrounded the property culminating in a massive arched entryway that announced the property and the year it was built in 1796.

The evening was cold and the moon shone bright as Dr. Hichcock walked the gravel path that led up to the house. The large living room windows were illuminated and he could see the silhouettes of Margareta, his lovely blonde wife, as she played the piano surrounded by a group of men and women in fancy dress.

Hichcock hesitated at the front door looking toward the window again then turned and quickly made his way to a secondary entrance that led through the basement to the back of the house.

As he was climbing the narrow back stairs to his bedchamber, Hichcock heard a noise. He looked up to see a small woman staring down at him from the second floor landing. She held a glowing oil lamp in her hand revealing a middle-aged woman with a dour pinched face that was difficult to interpret. Her graying hair was pulled back into a tight bun. She wore severe black clothing that covered almost all of her tiny frame. Her eyes were equally as black as her dress and they seemed to look through a person instead of at a person. She did not smile. She held no expression at all.

Martha opened her mouth slightly as if to speak, but was silent. She stood waiting for the doctor to address her. Hichcock did not stop his climb to the third floor, but his eyes did meet Martha's and he addressed her respectfully.

"Oh, Martha, please let my wife know that I'm back from the hospital, but that I'm very tired and am going to my room. I will not be socializing this evening"

Martha nodded and held the lamp up to light the doctor as he walked up the stairs. She said, "Yes ... everything is ready, Doctor."

"Thank you, Martha."

Hichcock entered his room tossing his coat and hat on a settee as he walked over to a large desk. On top of the desk was an ornate brass and glass oil lamp lighting up a tableau of research books and correspondence. The doctor picked up the letters and glanced at them, tossing them one by one back onto the desk.

He looked around the large room furnished with exquisite carved walnut furniture, his eyes resting on a magnificent oil portrait of his wife, Margareta, that stood over an unlit fireplace. He could hear the faint strains of Tchaikovsky's famous Piano Concerto No. 1 that came from the living room two floors below. His wife was an accomplished pianist and she found much delight in entertaining guests with her virtuoso performances.

The doctor made a gesture of impatience and threw the remaining letters back onto the desk. He picked up a book and opened it, staring at the page only for a moment until his brows furrowed. He let it drop back to the desktop with a dull thud.

Hichcock's hands held a slight tremor to them. He held them

before him and winced. Clasping them together, fingers enjoined, he squeezed them tightly against each other.

The large formal living room was very luxurious and filled with fine furniture. The cut glass chandeliers and oil lamps that were strategically placed around the room gave the setting a pale yellow sparkle.

A grand staircase led to the upper two floors. Landscape oil paintings adorned the walls of the living room and up the staircase. On one wall hung a life-size ornately framed portrait depicting the beautiful Margareta standing in a colorful English garden holding their cat, Jezebel, in her arms. She wore a white lace dress and white high-ankle boots. The black cat created a stark contrast against the white of Margareta's clothing.

Margareta Hichcock's eyes were fixed as if in a trance as she entered into the triumphal bridge passage of the concerto's third movement. The gleaming black grand piano was the focal point of the living room, but the face of the woman behind it was where every eye was focused. She held her audience spellbound. The only sound apart from the music was the whisper of the ladies' fans as they increased in speed to the tempo of the building crescendo.

Across from the piano and behind the onlookers a velvet curtain was pulled aside. The enigmatic face of Martha appeared. She kept her gaze on Margareta until she caught the woman's eye and then she gave a slight nod.

Margareta acknowledged the signal with a slight movement of her head to inform the housekeeper that she had received the message.

She continued to play until the end of the piece and then stood and smiled, curtseying to a rousing applause from the gentlemen and their ladies.

Dr. Hichcock was wrapped in a burgundy velvet lounging robe. He sat at his desk and flipped through a book without reading it.

Upon hearing the final notes of the concerto and the applause that followed, he threw the book on to the desk and ran to the door in order to hear better. His hands began to tremble as he heard Margareta's voice.

"If you will all excuse me, I am a little tired. I believe I will retire for the evening. Thank you for coming. You've been delightful guests. Please accept my apology that Bernard could not join us this evening. He was in surgery."

Margareta walked to the front door as her guests took up their coats, scarves, and hats. Someone said, "It's you who must forgive us. We have abused your kindness by overstaying our welcome this evening. I, myself, lost track of time!"

She dismissed the guests one by one as they exited into the cold of the October evening. Their departing words were all filled with kindness.

"You are so lovely, my dear. Bernard is fortunate to have you at his side."

"Goodbye. We will see you soon. Give our love to Bernard!"

"Farewell ... thank you for the concert!"

There were kisses and hugs all around until the last of them was out the door. She stood and watched them for a moment, her breath forming a small cloud of vapor in the air above her.

Hichcock licked his lips and rubbed his palms together. He crossed from the door to the window that looked out over the front of the house. He could see the guests leaving and his heart began to beat faster when he heard the front door close.

He walked to the desk and opened a locked drawer. From there he removed a small, ornately carved jewelry box, opened it, and took out a glass vial containing a brown liquid. His hands trembled as he held it up to the light to look at the contents.

He then crossed to the bedside table and placed a match to a three-arm candelabrum. Once lit, he took it up and left the room for the darkened staircase. The three candles threw the shadow of his figure, large and distorted on the narrow hall wall beside him.

A few steps down, Hichcock stopped, cocked his head slightly and listened. The house was silent. He continued until he came to the second floor landing. On one side was a full-length mirror and on the other a door.

A large black cat sat curled up before the door. Jezebel looked up at the doctor with anxious yellow eyes.

Hichcock bent down to pet the cat as it arched its back in a prolonged stretch and meowed.

"What is that, Jezebel? Are you feeling lonely this cold night?"

The cat stared at him and responded with a mournful meow that sounded more like a lamentation to the doctor.

He pulled a key from a pocket of his robe and opened the door. He nudged the cat with the toe of a shoe and the cat got up and moved. Hichcock entered the room with the candelabrum held high.

The room was filled with a parade of lighted candles in all shapes and sizes. Hichcock walked the room with a slow solemnity looking about him as he went. He sat the candelabrum on a table and picked up four large candles placing them at the corners of a mortuary viewing bed. The bed had ebony marble columns and black satin sheets.

The whole room was draped in funeral vestments, velvet, satin, and silk blacks with gilded edges. On top of the bed lay the beautiful Margareta. She wore only a sheer negligee and a smile.

The doctor looked down upon her reverently. His eyes dilated and his body quivered. Pulling his eyes away, Hichcock broke the vial he had taken from his bedchamber and quickly loaded a syringe. Margareta held her arm up to him in supplication, her eyes filled with love. Hichcock bent down and kissed his wife while he caressed her arm tenderly and then injected the brown fluid into her arm.

The anesthetic took effect almost immediately. Margareta relaxed and, in a moment, she had completely lost consciousness. Hichcock's temples pounded as he gazed down at his wife. He gently touched her lips with his fingertips while he caressed her face, moving down her chin and neck to caress the length of her.

Quite suddenly with a violent gesture, he tore the negligee from her naked body revealing the creamy flesh that goose-bumped in the chilly air.

CHAPTER THREE

How she then wore it on the brows,
Yet am I glad to have her dead
Here in this wretched wattled house
Where I can kiss her eyes and head.

Nothing is better, I well know,
Than love; no amber in cold sea
Or gathered berries under snow:
That is well seen of her and me.

The long sterile hallway was sanctioned off into individual areas by a series of starched curtains. Behind one such curtain lay a woman who slept serenely. She was tucked into a narrow hospital bed.

A number of people surrounded her bed. The imposing figure of Dr. Hichcock stood out from the rest as he stood back watching the students at work. A team of interns was busy around the bed. One took the woman's blood pressure. Another monitored her vitals. Two others stood and took notes.

The woman's eyes fluttered then opened and traveled the room until they found Dr. Hichcock. She smiled.

Her sister who had been seated jumped up and ran to her side. Tears streamed her face as she realized her sister was out of danger. She turned to the doctor and reached a hand out, taking his arm and drawing him close. Then she took both of his hands together and kissed them saying, "Thank you, Doctor! It's a miracle!"

Hichcock replied, "There is no need to thank me, thank science."

An assistant looked up from the bed and said, "It's a great victory, Professor. If it isn't a miracle, it certainly has all the hallmarks of one."

The physicians left the cubicle leaving the two sisters to their privacy.

Dr. Hichcock and his team walked the curtained corridor and discussed the success of his procedure on the woman.

Hichcock said, "The medical profession has lost a lot of time considering the soul to be the material part of our being. A rational mind should realize that it is still an unknown universe. It is time that we began taking care of the body apart from the soul."

A student scurrying to keep up, looked up from his notes and said, "And still, Professor, if you had not taken steps to slow the heart rate, the patient would not have survived. Is there no connection to the soul, the inner being, in such a treatment?"

Hichcock stopped and looked at the young man. Was he being challenged? He wasn't sure but he was not about to reveal too much of his theory just yet. He curtly replied, "It is clear that the anesthetic slows down the dynamics of the heart and quite possibly other organs as well. My study continues."

The Professor had spoken and his students looked at him with a mixture of admiration, thirst for knowledge, and fear.

Just then a nurse came running up to the group and said, "Dr. Hichcock, we have a patient in the operating room. You are needed at once!"

Hichcock turned to his small retinue and said, "Let's go!"

The operating room being used was quite different from the teaching amphitheater. It was small and cramped for the five men and a nurse that surrounded a bed on which lay a young woman.

Dr. Hichcock opened a cupboard and took out a small brown bottle and passed it to one of the assistants.

He said, "We will attempt to administer the dosage by mouth. No more than ten drops, for starters."

The intern calculated ten drops by dropping them into a

spoon. He handed it to the patient, who drank it.

Almost immediately she closed her eyes. The intern monitored her heartbeat. As he did, the woman's eyes reopened.

"It has no effect, Professor."

Hichcock nodded and said, "Then let us proceed as usual. The vial please."

Another intern took a vial full of a brown liquid from a drawer and handed it to Hichcock. The doctor held it up to the overhead light to check its clarity.

RUBENS HOUSE MORTUARY ROOM

Dr. Hichcock held the vial of brown liquid up to the light to check its clarity. Satisfied, he broke the cap and filled a syringe.

The room was black. Dozens of candles emphasized that blackness all the more as their placement up high and low illuminated the darkness.

Margareta lay upon the black mortuary bed. Her beautiful body was clothed in the sheer negligee and the chill of the room caused her nipples to stand erect through the thin material. Her eyes sparkled and she smiled excitedly at her husband who stood above her.

A multitude of twinkling lights danced off of the ebony columns that surrounded the bed. In the background, one of Emile Berliner's new inventions, the gramophone, played a slightly tinny version of Margareta's version of Beethoven's Piano Sonata No. 32 in C Minor.

Hichcock looked down at his lovely wife and smiled back at her. As he did so he injected the brown fluid into her arm.

Margareta closed her eyes. Hichcock allowed a few bars of the sonata to play before he placed his hands on his wife. He went to her breasts and cupped them, circling his palms lightly over the erect nipples. His body shuddered uncontrollably as he did so and his eyes glazed over as if in a trance.

Quite suddenly Margareta's eyes opened and then closed once again. Unsure, Hichcock broke away from his sexual fantasy to remove a second vial from his robe pocket. He prepared a second syringe and, with no hesitation, injected the fluid into her arm.

Before he had fully released the entire syringe, Margareta's body spasmed in the throe of a mighty seizure. She opened her mouth and gasped for breath but none came. Her eyes turned to fix upon her husband. They spoke the fear that she was unable to verbally utter. She contracted once more with a violent spasm and then collapsed to lie still.

Dr. Hichcock dropped the syringe and pounced on her. He listened to her heart then attempted to revive her by pushing on her chest with his palms and mouth-to-mouth resuscitation. All was to no avail.

With glazed eyes staring at her husband, Margareta gave one last tremor of her lips and then breathed her last breath.

Hichcock put his hands to his face and screamed in agony, totally overcome by guilt and hopelessness.

It was pouring rain. But the ancient English Baroque-styled building of St. Paul's Cathedral stood defiant against the weather. Three hundred and sixty-five feet in the air was its massive dome topped with a tall lantern that contained a cross sitting on a golden ball. The cross represented an atonement for sin.

And yet sin defiled the majestic building that day in the personage of Dr. Bernard Hichcock.

Margareta's coffin was carried out between the huge columns and down the concrete steps of the cathedral's west entrance. The rain ran in rivulets down the sides of the gleaming hardwood and gold trimmed coffin that was transported on the shoulders of four somber men in black.

Dr. Hichcock and the housekeeper, Martha, followed the men. Behind them were a train of friends, Hichcock's medical associates, and a sprinkling of students.

Once the procession passed the columns, it became a sea of umbrellas fighting a stiff breeze as rain swept sideways through the mournful walk to the carriage that was to take the coffin back to the Rubens House crypt.

As the coffin was slid into the back of the carriage, the glass oval on the coffin lid came into view. Behind the beads of water on the glass shown the beautiful sleeping face of Margareta Hichcock. A golden plaque on the side of the coffin read:

MARGARETA HICHCOCK 1855 - 1885

A common practice among the well-to-do in Victorian England was for estates to contain their own crypts. This was mostly a preventative measure against the almost continual desecration of graves and theft of bodies used for medical research. Although the Anatomy Act of 1832 did cut down on such activity by allowing the bodies of paupers to be studied without punishment, graves were still robbed and corpses were still being stolen to fulfill the great demand of the medical establishment.

Rubens House was built in 1796 and, as such, it had an underground burial crypt.

As the storm beat down on the old house, a carriage drove up the gravel driveway to stop before the front door.

The four pallbearers followed Dr. Hichcock down through the back basement entrance to a desolate room where the coffin was placed on a damp concrete slab that stood before a hole in the brick wall hinged with a rusty iron grate. They quietly spoke their condolences to Hichcock and departed. The other mourners were not invited and thus no one other than Hichcock and Martha were present.

The Hichcock crypt contained a few old coffins behind other grates in the wall. Several more had the grating open as if in an invitation to death.

The room was gloomy and dark. It was lit by a couple of oil lamps and a candelabrum. The brick and stone walls were mildewed in places and cobwebs covered the low ceiling beams and the four corners of the room. The room was damp and the low ceiling made it seem even more oppressive.

The coffin was wet and a weeping Hichcock lovingly rubbed it down to dry it before turning down the oil lamps leaving the candles to burn down on their own. In sadness, he left the room, tears streaming down his face.

The room was silent and the coffin sat forlornly atop the wet slab.

A rustle sounded followed by a whoosh and Margareta's large black cat, Jezebel, landed on top of the coffin. He licked the beads of water from the oval glass and when he saw his mistress behind the glass, the hackles stood on his back and he let out a long mournful cry.

Hichcock, tears glistening in his eyes, sat behind the desk in his bedchamber study as porters carried out his baggage. The doctor reviewed letters of correspondence and condolence notes before dumping them all in the trash bin beside the desk. He stood up slowly, his face a mask of pain.

The tiny figure of Martha dressed all in black entered the open room without knocking. Her face was drawn and her eyes red from crying. She stood at the door and watched Hichcock with great sorrow.

"The carriage is at the door, sir. You just decided to leave today?"

Hichcock did not look up. He adjusted the black mourning band on his right arm.

"Yes, Martha. Everything here reminds me of Margareta, everything. I resigned my position from the hospital. Please take care of her home."

Martha's face became its usual mask and she replied, "Absolutely, Doctor Hichcock."

"Goodbye, Martha."

"Goodbye, Doctor."

And then Hichcock stopped and turned, saying "Oh, Martha, do take care of the cat."

"Jezebel? I have not seen her since ... well, I will try."

CHAPTER FOUR

Three thoughts I make my pleasure of:
First I take heart and think of this:
That knight's gold hair she chose to love,
His mouth she had such will to kiss.

Then I remember that sundawn
I brought him by a privy way
Out at her lattice, and thereon
What gracious words she found to say.

The Daily Telegraph and Courier ran a headline in the Saturday, September 25, 1897 edition that read:

AFTER TWELVE YEARS ABSENCE DOCTOR BERNARD HICHCOCK RETURNS TO LONDON

A sleek black coach ran south along a dirt road in the English countryside of Highbury Hill. The coach bounced and careened on the uneven road and sent a cloud of dust behind as its driver sped it through the early evening hours.

The occupants of the coach were a newlywed couple. Dr. Hichcock sat with his new bride, Cynthia, a beautiful brunette in her late twenties.

Her big brown eyes played out over the flow of a darkening landscape as the driver pushed them towards King's Cross and Hichcock's home, Rubens House, in Mecklenburgh Square.

Dr. Hichcock had aged well. He had retained his aristocratic good looks and perhaps they were even accentuated even more with the gray that ran through the hair at his temples. His face had softened a bit but his demeanor was as rigid as it was twelve years earlier.

He sat straight-backed on the cushioned couch and showed no interest in the passing countryside. Rather his face was turned toward his new bride.

"I hope you will be happy at Rubens House, my dear."

Cynthia smiled and said, "Dear Bernard, I am happy anywhere as long as you're with me."

The doctor nodded, satisfied, and took a cursory glance out the window and said, "We should be almost there."

The coach stopped at the arched entryway to Rubens House. The driver levered the brake and climbed down from the driver's box to open the coach door.

Cynthia was filled with excitement as she looked over the expanse of gardens and the estate before them. In the gathering darkness it was difficult to tell much about the place except that is was imposing.

The driver took a moment to light his coach lanterns and then walked to the back of the coach where he began to unstrap the boot.

Dr. Hichcock jumped to the ground and offered a hand to his new wife. She took his hand and stepped lightly to the ground. Cynthia wore a stunning green velvet dress that draped down to her black-booted feet.

Hichcock turned to the driver who had removed one of the bags and said, "Never mind the rest of the luggage. We will retrieve the bags in the morning."

"As you say, guv'na. A very good evening to you and the missus!"

The driver got back up on the box and drove off into the night.

Hichcock took up the bag and walked over to the massive iron gate. He hesitated a moment, looking through the bars at the house that brought back visions from long ago, then he shoved a big key in the lock and turned it with some effort.

He pushed the gate open on creaking hinges and stood staring at his property.

Cynthia felt a chill and shivered. She walked up to her husband who seemed momentarily far away.

"Bernard...?"

Hichcock did not seem to notice her, but he did respond. His response, however, was not directed to her but rather to what was going on inside his head.

"I'll make my way once again."

Just as quickly he seemed to awaken from his reminiscing state of mind. He took a couple of steps into the garden and looked around. He seemed excited and called to Cynthia, "Come here, my dear!"

The large expanse of lawn and the once lovely gardens within were now full of weeds and overgrown with brambles, some of which prevented passage along the gravel driveway to the house.

Hichcock swore, "Damn! Nature is such a bloody tyrant! It took my Margareta years to build the gardens and now look at them! They are gone ... all for naught!"

Cynthia winced when she heard her husband mention his deceased wife in a possessive manner. However, she recovered quickly and said, "I am sure we can reclaim the grounds once again, Bernard! Have faith, my husband."

Hichcock did not respond. The couple moved forward into the garden. The branch of a blackberry bush caught the hem of Cynthia's skirt and she reached down and freed it with a jerk.

Hichcock pulled back a low hanging branch that blocked the driveway. As he did, Cynthia stopped and pointed at the house.

"Look, there's a light in the window!"

On the first floor, a window was illuminated with a soft yellow light. That light brought some of the building's façade out of the shadow. Even in disrepair, the mansion was still impressive. Ivy and a climbing rose ran along the front of the residence up and through the geometric patterned ironwork of the terraces.

Cynthia was afraid. Rubens House was a shambles in its unkempt state. Were it not for the light, the house would appear to be uninhabited and perhaps even haunted. She asked, "Who can it be?"

Hichcock replied, "Martha, my housekeeper."

A sudden flash of lightning blinded the couple, followed by a mighty crack of thunder. A few large drops of cold rain began to pelt the ground.

"Hurry, my dear, before the rain comes full force!"

Hichcock gave his hand to his wife and they rushed up the gravel drive toward the house.

Hichcock placed a key into the front door and pushed open the heavy oak door. The hinges creaked, as it swung open. He entered into the darkness of the entrance followed by Cynthia who bumped into a chair covered with a white cloth.

Another flash of lightning threw light into the large front window. It revealed what once was an immaculate living room to be a gloomy, dusty room full of white-sheeted furniture.

Hichcock walked over to the piano and pulled the sheet back. He lovingly caressed the black wood casing. He walked around to the keyboard and tapped out a couple of notes. The sound reminded him of Margareta. He began to shake inside. Regaining control, he turned toward Cynthia and said, "Just a moment, my dear. I'll give us some light."

He struck a match and lit an ornate oil lamp that cast an eerie glow on their environs.

Hichcock called out, "Martha! Martha!"

There was no answer.

Cynthia looked around the room. Everything had the air of having been long neglected. Cobwebs hung from the glass chandeliers and drapery. And the fine wood floors and rugs were so dusty that their footsteps could be traced from the front entrance.

A momentary flash shone through the living room window. It illuminated the life-size ornately framed portrait of the beautiful Margareta.

Cynthia asked, her voice a bit hoarse, "Is that her portrait?"

Hichcock turned to look at the painting and said, "Yes, it is of Margareta."

The lightning storm increased in intensity and loud thunder

shook the house and rattled the windows. Distressed, Cynthia shuddered and pulled her arms tight around her shoulders.

Hichcock looked over at his bride and said, "Come over here, Cynthia." He pulled one of the sheets back from a sofa and motioned for her to sit. "Come on. Wait here, dear. I'm going to look for Martha."

Cynthia sat on the edge of the couch, tense, scared. The doctor crossed the hall, calling out to the diminutive housekeeper. "Martha! It's Bernard! We're home!"

Cynthia called out to Hichcock, "Do not leave me here, Bernard, please!"

But the man insisted and the authoritarian tone of his voice kept her from saying anything further.

"Wait here, Cynthia!"

Something rubbed against Cynthia's boot and she screamed. Jezebel, now old and balding, came tearing out from under the couch and shot out into the middle of the floor, yellow eyes ablaze and her hackles raised, screeching at the intruders.

Hichcock recognized Margareta's old cat and called out to it, "Jezebel!" and to Cynthia, "No need to fear. It's Jezebel! She's still alive!"

Cynthia looked back at the cat that stood arched a few feet away. Her eyes were huge and she seemed repulsed by the animal. She said to her husband, "Your Jezebel nearly scared the life out of me!"

Hichcock ignored the comment, patted his leg and called out to the cat, "Jezebel! Come! Come over here!"

But the cat gave another screech and then turned and ran away. Hichcock looked back at his wife and said, "She's gone feral."

The couple looked up to see the little old housekeeper, Martha, standing on the formal staircase watching them. Her once graying hair was now completely white and pulled back tightly into a bun. She still wore what appeared to be the same black suit with very little flesh showing except her face and hands.

Hichcock called up to her, "Good evening, Martha!"

Upon his greeting, Martha continued down the stairs holding

up a silver candelabrum with three lighted candles. Her face was a mask void of expression and she showed no joy in seeing the master of Rubens House. She responded to Hichcock's greeting by saying in a flat, almost hostile voice, "Welcome back, Doctor." She gave no indication that Cynthia was in the house. Her eyes never left those of the doctor.

Hichcock said, "Martha, I'd like you to meet Cynthia, my new wife. Cynthia, this is Martha, the housekeeper."

Cynthia sought to gain Martha's attention and addressed her cordially, "It is a pleasure to meet you, Martha."

But her attempt was to no avail. The old woman ignored her and instead spoke to Hichcock saying, "Excuse the mess. I only had time to tidy the rooms upstairs once I knew you were coming. If you are hungry, I have prepared something for you to eat."

Cynthia knew the housekeeper had snubbed her. It was uncomfortable being in the woman's presence. She was already unsure how the two would be able to live in the same house together. She also knew that, for her husband's sake, she was going to have to try.

Hichcock turned his attention to his wife and said, "You must be hungry, dear."

"No, no, I'm just tired."

Martha spoke with no emotion and said, "I will now accompany the lady to her room."

AAIIIEEEEOOOOO...

As soon as she had spoken, the terrible scream came out of nowhere and echoed throughout the house. Cynthia, startled by the unexpected noise, ran terrified to her husband. She clung to his arm and stuttered out, "What . . . what was . . . that hideous cry . . . Bernard?"

Martha's face contracted into a grimace of pain. She answered, "Madam, it is my sister. For years, she has lived here in Rubens House with me. But tomorrow I will take her to the asylum. She is not well. She suffers with mental illness."

Martha kept her eyes fixed on the doctor who returned her stare with a fixed intensity. He said nothing to the old housekeeper but sought to calm his wife by taking her arm and saying, "It will be okay. I will escort you to your room, my dear."

He took the candelabrum out of Martha's hand and started up the grand staircase with Cynthia close to his side.

Once out of Martha's vision, Cynthia broke away from her husband and stopped. She looked at Hichcock questioningly and asked, "Why did Martha ignore me and then look at me so strangely?"

Hichcock appeared a bit taken back at his wife's question, but rebounded with, "My dear Cynthia, Martha may seem strange, but she is a very good housekeeper." He avoided his wife's uncomprehending gaze and continued to rise.

When Hichcock reached the second floor landing, he faced the full-length mirror and, to its left, the door to the mortuary room. He stopped and turned to allow Cynthia to follow. She looked at him, her eyes dark and hurt from his curt response. She shrugged her shoulders and rejoined him to walk to the third floor landing where Hichcock stopped before a door in the hallway.

"This is your room, Cynthia. Mine is opposite."

Hichcock opened the door and held the candelabrum up high to reveal a well-furnished room with a large Queen Anne bed dressed in white. The floor was covered with expensive Oriental rugs and a huge mahogany wardroom stood across from the bed. There was even a matching vanity with a gilded oval mirror. Floral watercolors and oil landscapes adorned the four walls. It was obviously a room designed by and for a lady.

Hichcock looked at his wife and smiled. He said, "When everything is put back in order, it will be more welcoming. You'll see."

Cynthia looked around and said, "It is beautiful, Bernard," and then she hesitated and added, "Was this her . . . room?"

Hichcock did not acknowledge her question. He sat the candelabrum on a bedside table and walked to the door.

Cynthia immediately regretted her question and said, "Bernard, please forgive me. This house gives me a strange feeling. I feel like a stranger here . . . unwelcome. I feel that everything is hostile to me. Even the cat!"

Hichcock walked up to his wife and caressed her cheek. He

said, "You're just tired. Tomorrow we will look over the house and grounds in the daylight and things will be much different. I'll have Martha pick up our luggage. If you need something, there is the bell." And he pointed to a small silver bell on the nightstand.

"Thank you, Bernard."

"Goodnight, my love."

"Good night."

Hichcock exited the room and closed the door behind him.

CHAPTER FIVE

(Cold rushes for such little feet—
Both feet could lie into my hand:
A marvel was it of my sweet
Her upright body could so stand).

'Sweet friend, God give you thank and grace;
Now am I clean and whole of shame,
Nor shall men burn me in the face
For my sweet fault that scandals them.'

Left alone, Cynthia sat on the big white bed and looked around the room while flashes of lightning illuminated the scene followed by bone-rattling claps of thunder.

Something was wrong in Rubens House, something that involved Martha and Bernard. That thought made her shudder and filled her with apprehension.

The diminutive Martha stood in the living room staring up at the large oil portrait of Margareta. She held Jezebel in her arms, caressing the big black cat that purred contentedly. Lighted by a candle on each side of the portrait, the low light made the eyes come alive and appear to glow with a sparkling beauty.

Dr. Hichcock appeared on the stairwell just above the landing and stopped to look at Martha.

Martha looked at him with reproach in her eyes but she said nothing.

The cat hissed angrily and seemed to bristle upon seeing her old master. Hichcock's gaze went to the portrait and then back to Martha, who continued to stare accusingly. He said not a word but turned on his heel and started on his way back upstairs.

Cynthia undressed from her traveling clothes and then realized that she had forgotten that her luggage had not been dropped earlier in the day. Martha was to pick it up on the morrow. What to do?

Nude, she walked over to a large chest of drawers and opened a drawer randomly. Fortunately, it contained nightclothes and she chose a sheer white negligee. She made a conscious decision not to think about the fact that the clothing had once belonged to her predecessor, Margareta.

She slipped into the thin material. The fit was perfect and the silk felt good to her body. She stepped over to the vanity mirror to view herself. The suppleness of her young body pleased her but her eyes and complexion were not what she had expected. Her eyes were large and held fright. Her skin was pale, whether from fright or going most of the day without food. She hoped that tomorrow would be a better day.

The storm raged outside. A noise banged against the glass of the windows. It sounded almost like a knock on the door.

Cynthia walked to the bed and took up the candelabrum and walked over to the windows. She pulled the floor length velvet curtains aside and looked at the windows. They seemed to be secure. They were streaked with rain but all seemed in order. She was just getting ready to go to bed when a sudden gust of wind slammed a branch against the glass and it banged again. She nearly jumped out of her skin, but then realizing it was nothing, she laughed at herself silently and sighed with relief.

Walking up to the windows, Cynthia looked out over the grounds that lit up again and again with the continual lightning strikes. The yard was in such disarray. She thought what a job she would have ahead of her getting things back into order, but that she would do just that.

Her thoughts were cut off suddenly when she thought that she saw someone in the garden. But that couldn't be possible. Not in the storm. She wiped her hand over a pane to clear it of her breath and looked closer.

She was not wrong. There was a figure in the garden. It appeared to be a woman wearing a white cape and hood walking not aimlessly but with seeming intent.

Cynthia stared, her heart beating fast.

The white shadow turned and, for a moment, in the light of a flash, it seemed that where there should have been the flesh of a face under the hood there was instead the chiseled and sunken features of a skull. But the vision was too fleeting; the light from the flash had dissipated and the crash of thunder that followed along with the pouring rain made the picture unclear.

Cynthia closed her eyes in fear and when she reopened them, the frightening image had disappeared.

Distressed, she turned from the window and walked back to the bed.

Behind her, a flash of lightning and a clap of thunder brought on another gust of wind and the branch banged hard against the windows. The latch must have given way and the windows flew open. A cold gust of wind filled the draperies, blowing them inward, and the candles were immediately snuffed out.

Cynthia came close to screaming, but regained her composure and ran to close the windows, fighting against the fluttering curtains and pelting rain.

With great effort, Cynthia strove to calm down. She ran back to bed and, still wet, slipped under the covers, closed her eyes, and tried to fall asleep. But her mind was wide-awake and she felt sleep would never come in Rubens House.

The sound of heavy, slow-moving footsteps approached her room and stopped before the door.

Frightened, Cynthia's eyes were fixed on the door as she held her breath. The brass doorknob turned, once, twice, and then stopped. Someone was trying to get in to her room, but the door was locked.

"Bernard . . . Bernard, is that you?" she called out, her voice shaking with dread.

There was no answer and, after a few moments, the sonorous footsteps started up again away from her door.

Cynthia took a deep, shuddering breath and sighed. Her body relaxed and she pulled the covers up over her nose leaving only her big dark eyes visible, scanning back and forth over the room. It would be a very long night.

Cynthia awoke to sunshine. She yawned and got up. She

walked over to the wardrobe and opened it. It was full of Margareta's clothing. She chose a fluffy white robe and wrapped herself up in it.

She walked into the formal dining room to see Hichcock sitting at the head of the dining table, breakfast before him. She approached her husband with a smile and he kissed her on the forehead. The man seemed cheery despite the previous evening's happenings and storm. He said, "Good morning, my dear!"

"Good morning," she responded with little enthusiasm. She dropped into the chair next to him.

"What's wrong?"

"I did not sleep well, Bernard."

"And why is that?"

Cynthia looked at him incredulously. She said, "You ... you didn't hear anything last night?"

Hichcock gave her a puzzled look and replied, pouring tea for the two of them, "No, nothing. I slept like a baby."

"After you left, someone tried to get into my room."

"Cynthia, that is absurd. I don't see how that could possibly be when it is just you, me, and Martha in the house."

"No . . . there is another, Bernard! There is her sister! The one who is sick . . . or insane!" She shuddered and took a sip of tea, the cup shaking in her hand. "I heard footsteps and saw the doorknob turn, but I had it locked."

Hichcock smiled at her as a father does to a frightened child and then shook his head.

"Cynthia, you were very tired last night, maybe you imagined it."

Cynthia stamped her foot and furrowed her brow. She sought his eyes and said, "No, you are wrong! There was someone outside my door, I'm sure of it!"

Hichcock sat down his cup with an annoyed gesture and said with an authoritarian tone, "Cynthia, my room is adjacent to yours and I heard nothing. Your nerves are getting the best of you!" He sighed and changed his tone saying, "I'm sorry, dear, coming back into this house after all these years has made me a bit nervous. I should not have snapped at you."

Husband and wife turned to look at Martha who arrived to stand at the entranceway to the dining room. She announced, "There is a nurse from the hospital, a Ms. Franz, and she wants to talk to you, Dr. Hichcock."

"Let her know I'll be right there, Martha."

Martha exited and he patted Cynthia's hand.

"It will be alright, dear. You must give it time."

He got up and followed Martha.

Cynthia bit into a croissant, but she had no appetite. She got up from the table carrying her tea into the living room and stood in front of the portrait of Margareta.

It was nothing more than a large portrait of a very pretty woman in a white dress holding a large black cat in a garden... perhaps a garden here at Rubens House. But there was something malevolent in the painting although Cynthia wasn't sure just what it was. It felt like the eyes of both Margareta and the cat, Jezebel, followed Cynthia's movements which she found unnerving.

Cynthia turned her back to the painting and walked over to look out the front window. The expansive view, if offered, was of a previously manicured front lawn. In the sunlight, it did not appear as menacing, just as Bernard had assured her. It was, rather, a desolate, weed and bramble-filled area that needed a lot of love and attention.

Cynthia shook her head unsure if at herself or her circumstances and turned to walk back into the dining room.

Had she stayed a moment longer at the window, she may have seen a branch move in the overrun garden, a branch that moved even though there was no wind and the garden appeared to be deserted.

Cynthia sat at the dining table drinking tea and contemplating her day when a tap came upon her shoulder. She jumped and spilled her tea on the lace tablecloth.

"Bernard, you frightened me! I didn't hear you come in!"

Hichcock smiled at his young bride and said, "I didn't mean to startle you, my dear. I have to rush straight to the hospital.

We're invited to the theater this evening. I will pick you up at seven o'clock. Please be ready."

Cynthia did not respond. She watched her husband leave. When she could no longer hear his steps, she got back up and went back to the painting of Margareta to examine it more closely. Margareta wore high collar white-laced boots, a white lace dress, and was crowned with beautiful blond curls that fell past her shoulders onto the dress. It was the gaze of her eyes ... that arrogance that was so unsettling.

As Cynthia examined the painting, a hissing seemed to come from the cat in the painting.

Cynthia stared at the likeness of Jezebel in the painting. It was just a painting. The hissing came again and she turned to see the big cat sitting on top of the piano watching her.

She attempted to approach the cat in a friendly manner, but the animal's hair bristled and it quickly turned and ran away. She shook her head and thought just how alone she was in Rubens House.

Regardless of her feelings, she must get on with her day. There was obviously much to do. She climbed the stairs leading to her bedchamber to get dressed and ready for the day.

One the second floor landing Cynthia stopped in front of the big mirror that was on the wall just opposite the stairwell. She then turned to the door of the room opposite. She tried the doorknob but the door was locked.

Without warning, Martha's hand grabbed her by the shoulder. Frightened, Cynthia turned to face the old housekeeper.

Martha's face showed no emotion, but her tone was full of venom. She said, "Your room is upstairs."

Cynthia asked, "Why is this room locked, Martha?"

"The master always keeps it locked."

Martha said nothing more, but continued her stare until Cynthia turned and hurried her climb up to the third floor and her bedchamber.

CHAPTER SIX

I tell you over word by word.
She, sitting edgewise on her bed,
Holding her feet, said thus. The third,
A sweeter thing than these, I said.

God, that makes time and ruins it
And alters not, abiding God,
Changed with disease her body sweet,
The body of love wherein she abode.

ROYAL VICTORIA HALL

The orchestra played the last few notes of the grand finale while the velvet curtains closed before the troupe of actors who were taking their bow. The audience rose from their seats and filled the theater with applause. The show was a rousing success.

Soon after, the foyer was a mass of elegantly dressed men and women, some praising and some critiquing the merits of the play and the various actors in it.

Cynthia was happy, walking alongside her husband and Dr. Kurt, a handsome young man just a few years senior to her own age. Kurt contrasted greatly with her husband. Visually he was not as tall, a bit broader in the shoulders, sporting a head of wavy black hair with long thick sideburns. He wore a black dinner jacket with a peaked lapel, cummerbund, and bow tie rather than the traditional English coat and tails that her husband wore.

There was an amicable openness about Kurt that made him immediately likeable and she was glad he had accompanied her and Bernard to the theater. His presence gave some semblance of normality to what had been a most abnormal and unnerving couple of days.

Cynthia smiled and said, "The play was so enjoyable. The orchestra was outstanding!"

Hichcock replied, "Yes, wonderful show."

Cynthia sought to bring Dr. Kurt into the conversation addressing him directly by asking, "Was the play to your liking, Dr. Kurt?"

Kurt laughed and replied, "Yes, very much! Too bad the soprano was fat and a bit long in the tooth."

Cynthia laughed with him.

A moment later, a theater attendant made his way through the crowd and approached Hichcock. The boy whispered something in his ear, Hichcock nodded and handed him a coin in return. The doctor then turned to his wife and Dr. Kurt.

"I have to go to the hospital right away. It is most unexpected. I'm sorry dear." He looked directly at Kurt and said, "Would you mind accompanying Cynthia home and then meeting me at the hospital?" and back to his wife, "I will be home as soon as possible, dear. Dr. Kurt will see that you get home safely."

Cynthia wasn't sure if she was hurt or not. She was confused that her husband would leave her alone in the company of a total stranger. She responded, "I hope to see you later, Bernard."

Dr. Kurt gave a look of concern to the older physician and said, "Of course, Doctor. I will see Mrs. Hichcock home and meet you at the hospital just as soon as possible!"

Hichcock turned and disappeared into the crowd leaving the two strangers as new companions.

Kurt shrugged his shoulders and looked at his lovely companion with a mischievous grin. He said, "Shall we?"

Cynthia took his arm and they made their way through the crowd to hail a hackney coach for the ride back to Rubens House.

The hackney crossed over the River Thames via Blackfriars Bridge en route back to Mecklenburgh Square. The horse's hooves clacked on the Portland stone roadway and his breath blew puffs of warm air that rapidly chilled as the cabbie sang to him softy.

Dr. Kurt pulled the blanket over their legs and smiled at

Cynthia. He said, "I was in Vienna when I learned that your husband had started teaching at University Hospital here in London. I sought a transfer immediately in hopes of being able to work with him. His experiments have always fascinated me greatly. I remember reading that he had transplanted the entire face of a woman who had been burned beyond recognition! No one has ever accomplished such a feat before."

Cynthia nearly gagged inwardly, but gave Kurt a look of appreciation and replied, "Oh, I've heard that the true charm of a medical mind can take a lifetime to appreciate."

Kurt paused a moment and said, "Charm...? I would say a medical mind must be dedicated to his or her profession and that great accomplishments often take a lifetime to achieve."

Cynthia started, "What I meant—"

But Kurt wasn't finished. He passionately interrupted with, "Mrs. Hichcock, in Vienna I studied with Professor Freud, a man not unlike your husband in certain respects. Have you heard of him?"

"No . . . and please call me Cynthia."

There was a moment of awkward silence between the two and then Kurt looked at Cynthia in the eyes and confessed, "Once I admired Professor Hichcock, now I must confess that I envy him."

Cynthia looked at the young physician coyly, smiled, dropped her eyes and said, "Thank you, Dr. Kurt."

"Edward..."

"Thank you, Edward."

The coach stopped in front of the arched entrance gate to Rubens House. The landscape was draped in fog and it was difficult to see beyond the wall and gate.

Kurt opened the door, hopped down, and reached his hand up to assist Cynthia in exiting the coach. He said, "Cynthia, I hope my prattling on has not bored you."

"No, far from it, Edward."

"Would you allow me to walk you to the door?"

"No, thank you. You better not. My husband is waiting for you at the hospital. Remember?"

Kurt nodded and walked with her the few feet to the gate. He kissed her hand, gave a short bow and said, "Good night ... Cynthia."

"Good night, Edward, and thank you."

Cynthia opened the gate and entered the estate grounds. She turned around to see Kurt walking back to the hackney saying, "University Hospital, driver!" After Kurt climbed into the coach, the driver snapped the reins making a clicking sound and the horse started up, carrying them off into the night.

After closing the gate behind her, Cynthia looked toward the house. It was unlit and the fog was so thick that it was difficult to see much further than a few feet ahead. Why had she been so foolish to turn down Edward's offer to walk her to the door?

She was afraid, but there was nothing to be done about it. She simply had to proceed slowly and she would make it.

As she started to move forward, Cynthia heard a slight rustle among the leaves and branches to her left. She stopped in her tracks and listened intently.

A low guttural female voice came from behind the overgrown bramble bushes in the yard. The voice said, "I'll get you in your sleep ... in my sleep ... I . . . am . . . death!"

Cynthia ran toward the house. She felt something take hold of her. She cried out but she didn't stop. Her skirt tore and a branch swatted her in the face, but she ran on up the gravel drive, her heart beating madly.

The voice seemed to follow her. It said, "I am death . . . DEATH!" The words ended with a fit of cackling laughter that seemed to come from all around her and then, silence.

Suddenly Cynthia spied a glow in front of her. It moved and was approaching her from the house. A small, shadowed figure came into view in the yellow glow of the light. A moment later, Martha emerged from the thick mist with an oil lamp held aloft.

She stopped directly in front Cynthia and the tiny black clad housekeeper said, "Ah, it's you! I heard a noise and came to see what it was."

Cynthia sobbed, "Martha, please, please, help me to the house!"

The housekeeper showed no concern for her mistress. Her face was a featureless mask. She turned her back to Cynthia and said, "Come on... this way," and led the way back along the drive to the front door.

Once inside the great house, Cynthia fell into a chair that had since been uncovered in the living room. She held her head in her hands and wept.

Martha stood before and after a moment said, "The master will be late this evening. You should go to bed."

Cynthia looked up. Tears streaming down her face, she said with no emotion, "Yes, of course," and got up to follow Martha upstairs.

As they walked to the grand staircase, Martha stopped to look at the portrait of Margareta. She held the oil light high to throw more light on the painting.

Cynthia stared at Martha incredulously. Martha turned her eyes toward Cynthia and the two women exchanged hostile glances. Then Cynthia held out her hand for the oil lamp the little old woman held.

The housekeeper passed the lamp to her and turned to walk off.

But Cynthia's next words stopped her.

"Martha, you are dismissed for the evening. But before you go, tell me when you will have your sick sister out of Rubens House."

"My sister, Mrs. Hichcock? She was admitted to the asylum just as I told you she would be... this very morning." Martha turned and walked off.

Cynthia stood on the bottom rung of the stairs for a moment, her brows furrowed, perplexed. Finally, she turned, held the light up high, proceeding up the flight of stairs.

Cynthia entered her room and placed the oil lamp on the nightstand beside the bed. She thought back to the handsome young man, Dr. Edward Kurt, who had accompanied her home and she smiled to herself. She removed her coat and slipped out of her ruined dress. She walked to the mirror and viewed herself. Her face carried a red welt where the branch had slapped her across the face. Her eyes were red, her face streaked, and she looked pallid and haggard. Her calves were scratched from running through the brambles.

She shuddered and hugged herself arms crossed over her breasts, then walked over to the bed and pulled down the covers.

A human skull sat atop one of the bed pillows.

Cynthia screamed and fainted.

CHAPTER SEVEN

Love is more sweet and comelier
Than a dove's throat strained out to sing.
All they spat out and cursed at her
And cast her forth for a base thing.

They cursed her, seeing how God had wrought
This curse to plague her, a curse of his.
Fools were they surely, seeing not
How sweeter than all sweet she is.

The operating room was crowded. Dr. Hichcock, Dr. Kurt, two interns, and a nurse stood almost shoulder-to-shoulder around the operating table that held the body of a middle age woman. Hichcock's smock and gloves were covered with blood as he stood back from the table. The room was silent.

One of the interns monitored the pulse of the patient. Finally, he looked up and shook his head. The nurse pulled the starched white bed sheet over the face of the deceased and went about the process of sterilizing the surgical utensils.

Dr. Hichcock stripped off his surgical gloves and let them fall to the floor, his face dark and his brows heavily furrowed.
The two interns stood in the corner of the small room taking notes. They whispered to one another, commenting on the surgery.

"Did you notice? The Professor is not the same man he once was."

"No, he isn't. He left her to die when he could have saved her."

Dr. Kurt looked at Hichcock with concern. He seemed to be struggling with indecision as he started to speak, stopped, and then started again.

"Professor, why . . . ah ... Professor Hichcock, why did you not use the anesthetic you perfected? Perhaps it would have saved her life."

Hichcock replied dully, "Perfected...? No, I will never use the anesthetic again. It is not perfected and I do not think it ever will be. It has proven to be fatal..."

"But you've saved many—"

Hichcock did not wait for the reply. He turned and quickly exited the room, leaving Dr. Kurt to wonder what was wrong with his mentor.

Dr. Hichcock stood alone in the hospital physician's lounge. He had removed the bloody smock and wore the immaculate coat and tails he had been wearing to the theater earlier in the evening. He stood before a bar and poured three fingers of gin into a glass, throwing it down in a single gulp.

He slammed the glass down hard and a violent shudder traveled through his body. Hichcock sat down in one of the overstuffed lounge chairs in order to regain his calm, his hands trembling slightly. He held them out before him and whispered to himself, "No, nooooo...!" In frustration, he closed his eyes and clasped his hands together, enjoining his fingers and squeezing them tightly against each other.

After a while, Hichcock got up and with great strides left the lounge.

Three floors underground, approachable from a steep winding staircase or a large pulley lift for transporting bodies, the University Hospital mortuary was built with whitewashed stone and slate flooring. The room was chilly and, while not optimal for long-term preservation, the cadavers generally lasted long enough for burial or, if unclaimed, dissection for the enlightenment of the university's students and for scientific study.

Dr. Hichcock walked hurriedly down the staircase until he came to the door with the word MORTUARY lettered on it. He stopped, undecided, seemingly tormented within, and then turned to retrace his steps up the stairs. Hichcock took a few steps and then paused and held his head in his hands. He turned once more and walked back to open the door.

Once inside and just to the right of the door stood a table that held two oil lamps. Hichcock struck a match and lit the one closest to him, turning up the wick to throw as much light as possible into the dark, frigid room.

Before him, a stretcher lay on top of a sturdy table. The corpse of the middle age woman he had unsuccessfully operated on earlier was upon the stretcher. The nurse or some attendant had cleaned the body and pulled back the hair to frame the face, giving it a sense of peace.

Hichcock walked up to the body and sat the lamp on the table beside the stretcher. He looked down at the seemingly sleeping figure clothed in a white hospital gown and his eyes began to dilate and his breathing became heavy and ragged. A weird expression distorted the doctor's face, one of perverted animalistic desire and an excitement that made his hands tremble beyond control.

The doctor reached out his hands and lifted the gown away from the woman's body. He placed his fingers on the ruby nubs of her nipples and sighed deeply as he caressed the large breasts. His hands then began their journey of exploration in places his scalpel never touched.

Quite suddenly, the door opened and a voice called out, "Hullo . . . who's there? Oh, Professor, I'm sorry! Do you need anything?"

Hichcock looked up and fixed a glassy-eyed, uncomprehending glance upon an elderly man standing in the doorway, mop and bucket in hand. Then Hichcock looked back down at the body before him then back up at the old janitor. By now recovered, he did not answer the old man, but rather just shook his head as if to indicate nothing was needed.

The janitor turned, appearing to pay no mind to what he saw, and closed the door shut behind him. Hichcock replaced the gown upon the corpse, ensuring all was as he had found it, then walked to the door, dousing the lamp as he exited the room.

Cynthia opened her eyes to the ceiling of her room. She was cold and naked, lying on the floor beside the bed. Confused, she blinked a couple of times and then stood up.

She looked back at the bed and all was as it should be. The large mahogany bed was dressed all in white linens and blankets and the pillows were fluffed just so. Cynthia lifted the sheets to peer under them, fearing the worst, but the skull was gone.

She stood looking at the empty pillow. Who had removed the skull? And for that matter, who had put it there in the first place? She put a palm to her forehead and the thought occurred that she might be having hallucinations.

She heard the sound of footsteps outside her door. They were not as heavy as the one she heard before. A woman's?

Cynthia quietly walked to the door and stooped down, putting her eye to the keyhole. In the narrow opening, she saw the lower part of a figure walk past. It was that of a woman wearing the same white high-collar lace-up boots and the hem of a white lace dress showed just above them.

The woman walked to the stairway and then turned back towards Cynthia's room. Cynthia nearly fainted again but consciously slowed her breathing and checked to make sure the door was locked. It was.

Cynthia walked to the wardrobe and slipped into a robe, then went and sat in the chair by the window to wait out the remainder of the night.

CHAPTER EIGHT

He that had held her by the hair,
With kissing lips blinding her eyes,
Felt her bright bosom, strained and bare,
Sigh under him, with short mad cries.

Out of her throat and sobbing mouth
And body broken up with love,
With sweet hot tears his lips were loth
Her own should taste the savour of,

Bernard Hichcock stood at the window of his bedchamber, looking over the ruins of what used to be a magnificent lawn and garden. He wore a plum smoking jacket over light gray pajamas.

The morning's eastern light poured into the room and Cynthia had to squint to see her husband clearly at the window. She was clothed for the day but her features were not of the young vibrant woman who had entered Rubens House a few days earlier. She was pallid and haggard with dark eyes that seemed too large for her face.

"Bernard, I am sure of it! I know who it is too! I will never forget the vision of fear that is carved into my mind! You must believe me!"

Hichcock turned from the window and walked over to a painting of Margareta very similar to the one in the living room below. As he looked at it, his brows furrowed and he seemed annoyed. Finally he turned to Cynthia, snorted and said, "Cynthia, this is ridiculous! I have known you since your sickness. The shock over your father's death played havoc with your nervous system. I thought you were healed, but it is obvious to me that you are still suffering from delusions related to the trauma you experienced."

Cynthia pleaded with her husband in an effort to obtain some form of compassion from the man.

"I know it sounds absurd. But I am not crazy. I know what I saw. And it is not the first strange incident in this house. I nearly died of fright. I don't know how much more I can handle, Bernard!"

Hichcock did not respond. He walked to his desk and opened a humidor, selecting a cigar and lighting it, then looked up and blew a stream of smoke to the ceiling.

Cynthia bowed her head, hurt by the indifference of her husband, and said, "I waited for you all night, Bernard. I did not sleep. Where were you?"

"I came home very late."

The answer did not meet Cynthia's expectations and she approached her husband in supplication, her voice pleading, "All of these paintings of her ... even here in your room ... I know that you adored Margareta, but please try to understand, everywhere I go in this house, her eyes seem to follow my every move. I . . . I am your wife now, Bernard! Please love me...!"

Hichcock appeared nervous and he did not make eye contact with his young wife. Instead, he cut her plea for understanding and love short. He said harshly, "I am not going to discuss this any further with you. I have to go. Now go to your room, Cynthia!"

He walked to the bedchamber door and opened it, starting to leave, then turned and said, "Oh, Cynthia, remember when I am not home, I do not want anyone to come into this house."

Cynthia said nothing, but followed her husband through the door out into the hallway. His features were hard and cruel and he gave not a hint of indication that love had been a part of the still new marriage.

" I will see you at dinner."

Cynthia nodded and turned to the door of her room. She waited for the echo of his footsteps down the stairwell to fade before she tiptoed down without a sound. She stopped a few feet before the second floor landing, her back flat against the wall, and listened intently.

After a few minutes, Martha came up the stairs from below

and stopped in front of the full-length mirror that faced the stairwell on the second floor landing. The diminutive housekeeper carried a tray covered with a silver lid. She reached up a hand and turned an empty wall sconce. The mirror slid open like a pocket door. It was dark inside but Cynthia thought she saw some steps leading down unto the bowels of the old house. Martha entered into the narrow hallway and the mirror closed in behind her.

Cynthia eased her way down the remaining steps to stand in front of the mirrored doorway. She was tempted to follow Martha's actions and turn the sconce when, suddenly, a bell sounded below signifying someone was at the front door. The mystery would have to wait.

Cynthia opened the door to face a smiling Dr. Edward Kurt.
"Good morning, Cynthia!"
Cynthia's spirits lifted immediately upon seeing her new friend.
"Good Morning! Please do come in, Edward!"
Kurt entered and bowed, kissing her hand. She took his coat and hat and hung them beside the door.
"To what do I owe the honor of this visit?"
"Ah, actually I need to speak with your husband."
"I'm sorry, but if you did not see my husband outside, I am not sure exactly where he is. He's not in. Is it something urgent?"
"No, it's nothing urgent."
The living room had been cleaned and was now back in spotless order. She walked him to it and said, "Please, have a seat."
"No, thank you. But I do have a question for you, Cynthia. Are you happy here in London?"
Cynthia did not respond. She approached the young doctor with her eyes on the floor, uncertain. When she stood before him Kurt looked puzzled and asked, "Please, Cynthia forgive my impertinence—"
Cynthia interrupted and said in a matter-of-fact tone, "Doctor, do you believe in ghosts?"

"No, of course not. Why? What is the matter Cynthia?"

"Me, neither, until yesterday. Since I've been in this house, I have been living in fear. I'm not sure what to believe anymore, Edward. Yesterday I saw with my own eyes through the keyhole in my door the hem of a dress and boots ... like the ones in that painting." She pointed to the magnificent portrait of Margareta that hung near the stairway. "She was the first wife of Bernard. Her name was Margareta."

Kurt looked at Cynthia with compassion. As a physician whose expertise was surgery, his mind dealt well with rational facts but struggled with things that appeared irrational. Such were her words.

"Cynthia, what are you implying? Surely you are not suggesting the house is haunted! It must have been a hallucination ... a dream perhaps!"

She said softly, "I know it's hard to believe, but I'm telling you the truth, Edward."

Kurt explored her eyes for a moment, but said nothing.

Cynthia continued, "Would you be honest with me? Do you not find Bernard to be a bit strange?"

Kurt gave a slight cough into his hand and said, "Dr. Hichcock is a genius and all geniuses see the world a little bit differently than you and I. Why do you ask?"

"Oh, it was just a silly idea."

Cynthia lowered her head, and then, in a tone of courtesy said, "Edward, my apology. I forgot. Would you like something to drink? Some coffee?"

Kurt took her hands in his and said, "No, dear lady, thank you! I must get back to the hospital. Please give my regards to your husband."

Cynthia withdrew her hand, her face red with embarrassment.

As they walked back to the front door Kurt said, "If I can be of any assistance to you, Cynthia, please do not hesitate to let me know."

"Thank you, Edward."

She opened the front door and Kurt took up his coat and hat. He kissed her hand once more and looked into her eyes, trying to understand their strange conversation, but to no avail. Cynthia turned her head to avert her eyes. He placed his hat at a jaunty angle, smiling at her, and left the house.

CHAPTER NINE

Yea, he inside whose grasp all night
Her fervent body leapt or lay,
Stained with sharp kisses red and white,
Found her a plague to spurn away.

I hid her in this wattled house,
I served her water and poor bread.
For joy to kiss between her brows
Time upon time I was nigh dead.

Bernard and Cynthia Hichcock sat facing each other in the soft glow of candlelight. The living room was warm and inviting if it were not for the suffocating tenseness that crackled in the air between the two.

Hichcock seemed nervous. His hands had a tremor as he turned the pages of the Daily Telegraph and Courier. He couldn't concentrate and finally in frustration he folded the newspaper and got up and walked over to the portrait of Margareta and stood.

Cynthia was crocheting, but her mind was elsewhere. She, too, was tense and, every so often, she would look at her husband sideways in an effort to determine his state of mind.
She was terribly unhappy, but determined to make the best of the situation in which she found herself. As such she broke the silence and said, "Bernard, you seem distracted. Are you okay?"

Hichcock replied, "I have to go to the hospital."

"What...? Must you go, dear?"

He made no eye contact, but kept his eyes on the painting.

"Yes, I have some post-surgical follow-ups with a few patients and I must make my rounds before dawn."

"You are so changed. I feel that I mean nothing to you, Bernard." She looked beyond Hichcock to the painting he still faced and said, "Perhaps it was a mistake to bring me here."

"Nonsense, dear. I'm just a bit nervous. My hands are not as skilled as a few years back and it has me on edge."

Cynthia laid aside her crocheting then stood up and walked over to her husband. She took his hands in hers and looked up into this eyes saying, "Do not be late . . . tonight. I'm scared when I'm alone. Bernard . . . please!"

"Do you want me to ask Martha to sleep with you tonight?"

Cynthia's face blanched and she withdrew her hands. She shook her head and said, "No, not Martha! It is my husband I need. I do not want anything to do with Martha! I prefer to be alone!"

"Whatever you say, dear."

"Will you look in on me when you return?"

"I will come and say good night when I return."

To Cynthia it seemed her husband's words sounded hollow as if he were pacifying her. Knowing her fear of Martha perhaps his words were even a veiled threat. Nothing in her life was as it should be and she was confused.

Hichcock turned and left her standing alone.

Cynthia stood very still looking at the hated painting. She still had the feeling that Margareta was looking back and it was unnerving. Lost in thought, Cynthia was startled when Jezebel appeared on the stairs and hissed at her. Cynthia whirled to see the cat's big yellow eyes full of evil just before it bounded away.

Cynthia hadn't noticed because her eyes had been focused on the cat, but Martha stood on the stairwell where the cat had been. The tiny old woman was hard to see in her severe black clothing. She said nothing as she just stood there watching Cynthia, Martha's face a mask except for the eyes that held a controlled violence which terrified Cynthia.

Cynthia turned and ran from the room in an effort to free herself from eyes that followed her every move.

University Hospital was quiet after ten o'clock in the evening. The student interns and nurses took over, checking vitals and looking in on sleeping patients and otherwise maintaining status quo until morning when the full faculty of teaching physicians would be on the premises.

Far underground, the hospital mortuary was even quieter during the late evening hours. Unless a body had to be brought down via the lift, there was no need for the room to be in use. Bodies were brought up for dissection during daylight school hours only.

Dr. Hichcock approached the door to the mortuary and looked about him. The dark hallway off the room was silent and void of life.

He opened the door and lit an oil lamp that sat on the table next to the doorway.

Drawing the light up high, Hichcock walked up to several stretchers that held bodies. One held the body of a young boy, a drowning victim, the face blue and eyes bulging. Another stretcher held an elderly man whose heart had given out at a dinner party. He was dead on arrival at the hospital and was still clothed in his eveningwear. Hichcock thought that should make it easy on the mortician.

The third contained the body of a young woman. Hichcock lifted the sheet aside that covered the corpse. The body was beautiful and showed no signs of death. The long, curly blonde hair fell about the lovely face and shoulders in ringlets and the flesh appeared pink and still supple. It seemed to Hichcock that the woman was merely sleeping. Yes, she merely slept.

Hichcock's eyes dilated and his breathing became rapid. His hands trembled and he grasped them together, rubbing them to regain circulation and his composure.

His eyes traveled the length of her perfect body, the feet clean and delicate, the taut calves and thighs, the soft blonde curls of her womanhood, the concave waist, and the small, firm breasts that revealed a still youthful body.

The doctor's entire six-foot frame twitched in a sudden paroxysm of feverish delight and his hands unclasped to caress the cool flesh that lay before him. He bent close to smell her scent as he touched and fondled all of her.

The door opened. Dr. Edward Kurt stood with an oil lamp held high and his face was one of bewildered astonishment at what he faced.

Hichcock looked up to see the younger man's expression. He strove to compose himself and took the defensive. His tone was one of aggression as he asked, "Dr. Kurt, what are you doing here?"

The younger man still at a loss uttered, "I'm doctor-on-call. Surely you knew that, Professor. The hospital is quiet this evening and I was patrolling the facility. I heard a noise down here and a light where there should be neither. I did not expect to find you here."

Hichcock, now under full control, said, "Yes, well . . . I just wanted to check on the status of this patient's coagulation."

"Professor, I am the on-call physician. You could have called me. I would have helped."

"Dr. Kurt, I didn't know you were on duty tonight. However, this is not urgent. It can wait until morning. Come on, let's get out of here."

Hichcock doused the oil lamp, replaced it on the table and left the mortuary room. Kurt walked up to the body that his mentor had stood over and looked down at it. He wondered why was she completely uncovered and where were the Professor's medical instruments if he was checking for coagulation? He stood for a moment, perplexed, and then pulled the sheet back up to cover the corpse before he left the room.

CHAPTER TEN

Bread failed; we got but well-water
And gathered grass with dropping seed.
I had such joy of kissing her,
I had small care to sleep or feed.

Sometimes when service made me glad
The sharp tears leapt between my lids,
Falling on her, such joy I had
To do the service God forbids.

Cynthia sat in the chair by the window in her bedchamber reading a book by candlelight. The dance of the flames was more interesting than the book and soon they carried her thoughts to the mystery of Rubens House. The place was a house of secrets and she wanted answers . . . she needed answers to assure herself of her own sanity.

She must have dozed because suddenly she jumped when she heard the sound of a door slamming somewhere below. She closed the open book in her lap and placed it on the table and sat still listening for a sound.

She was now wide awake. The small pendulum clock said two forty-five and Bernard had not come to her yet. Taking up the candelabrum, Cynthia walked to the door and placed her ear to it, listening intently. She heard nothing.

Summoning up courage she cracked the door open and looked out. The hallway landing appeared to be empty. She eased out into the hall and closed her door behind her.

Without a sound, Cynthia made her way down the first flight of stairs to the second floor landing that held not one but two secret rooms. She stood in front of the mirrored doorway for a few minutes and listened for any sound within the house. When she felt assured no one was near and watching, Cynthia placed a hand upon the empty wall sconce and turned it as Martha had.

The mirrors slid open into pockets and a narrow staircase led down into the darkness. Cynthia was now running on pure adrenalin. Her heart beat faster, but her quest for answers was greater than her fear. She stepped into the doorway and it slid closed behind her.

Cynthia held the candelabrum up high and the light flickered in the airy stairwell. She walked down a flight of stairs and came to a landing. A door faced her and she tried the doorknob. It was locked. She continued down another flight of stairs and guessed that she was now somewhere below Rubens House. The air was decidedly chillier and she noticed dampness to the walls.

At the bottom of the second set of stairs, Cynthia came to a rusty metal gate. It did not appear to be locked. Cynthia pulled on it and it opened with a creak of the hinges. She stopped the moment the sound came and waited to make sure she heard no other sounds.

Once she felt she was alone, Cynthia entered and found herself in an unfinished earthen and stone tunnel. Massive stone blocks served as support for the ebony beams that held the ceiling in place. The breeze that passed through the twisting tunnel made the candles flicker and toss fantastic shapes onto the uneven red walls that surrounded her. Cobwebs brushed her face and clung to her clothing and Cynthia feared she would soon lose her nerve.

Finally she found herself facing a second metal gate. Cynthia did not pass it, but raised the candelabrum up high to light up the scene ahead of her.

It was a crypt. The ceiling was low and it seemed to be made entirely of brick and polished stone. Iron grates were fixed in the walls and blackness lay behind them. A few were open and stone shelves contained coffins in various states of decay whether through time or the dampness that permeated throughout the oppressive room. A skull had fallen out of one of the coffins and lay on its side on the floor, covered with webs, a haven for spiders.

A rat came from behind the skull, stopped and stared at the

light, and then scurried quickly across the floor to disappear behind one of the grates. Cynthia jumped and sucked in her breath when the rodent ran. She looked down and turned, shining the light at the ground around her to make sure there were no more rats close-by.

A single coffin sat atop a prominent stone slab in the center of the room. An empty grate was open just beyond and Cynthia wondered why the coffin had not been put away as the others had.

Cynthia attempted to open the gate to the crypt, but it was rusted closed and wouldn't budge. There was a reason that coffin had not been put away. It was more modern in design than the others in the room and, while everything in the crypt was covered with dust and mildew, the coffin looked as if it had been placed there only yesterday. The wood glowed in the candlelight and the handles and hinges were rust free.

Cynthia was full of dread. She knew with all of her being that the coffin held the body of Margareta.

The dull thud of a door closing somewhere behind her and a sudden gust of wind that snuffed the candles caused a cry of fear to escape Cynthia's throat.

Cynthia had forgotten to bring matches when she left her room so she would have to make her way out of the tunnel in the dark. She took a deep breath in an attempt not to lose control. She shook the gate again but it was stuck fast so she would have to retrace her steps back the way she had come.

Cynthia turned around and placed a hand on the wall and began to grope her way through the tunnel, her face and clothing a magnet for the cobwebs that hung all around her. A half-hour later she found herself lost and was close to sitting down, hoping that daylight would bring some light into the tunnel. Suddenly, she spotted a reflection ahead of her, higher and to her right.

She kept her eyes focused on the light and one hand on the wall and followed a path that traveled upward until a few minutes later she came to a small landing with what felt like wood under her feet. A door was ajar before her and it cast a little light to her surroundings.

Cynthia heard sounds coming from beyond the door. She

silently crept up to the opening and peered inside.

The room was not dirt and rock as in the tunnel she had just walked blindly through. It was a fully furnished room as if a part of Rubens House above. There were ornately framed paintings on the walls and it was filled with heavy antique furniture. The room had a chandelier, but was lit with a number of candlesticks placed around the room.

In the center of the room sat a high-backed chair with its back to Cynthia. She could see a glimpse of gray hair that fell over the back of the chair.

A moment later, Martha entered through a side door with a silver tray in her arms. She sat it down on an end table next to the high back chair, uncovered it, and handed a cup of tea to the person in the chair. As she did, she reached up and lovingly touched the hair of the figure.

Martha's eyes seemed to sparkle and a smile broke her normally emotionless countenance.

Cynthia withdrew quietly and made her way up a stairwell that was just beyond the doorway. The stairwell zigzagged and eventually led her back into the narrow stairwell she had originally entered into from the second floor landing. Once Cynthia entered this area, she could see light ahead and it made her passage easier. A few minutes later she exited into the hallway through the mirrored pocket doors that were now open.

Upon exiting onto the landing, she faced her husband who stood just beyond the door with a lit candelabrum, silent, as if waiting for her.

Cynthia's eyes grew large and she brought her hands to her chest as if to slow her rapid heartbeat.

Husband and wife's eyes fixed upon one another, but neither said a word. Cynthia turned and fled upstairs to her room.

Hichcock followed.

He came into the darkened room behind her just as she was lighting the oil lamp beside her bed. She tuned to face him.

Hichcock's face was hard and his lips turned down cruelly as he said, "I came to wish you a good night. Where have you been?"

Cynthia picked up the oil lamp and backed away from her husband. As she did she said, "Bernard, Martha did not tell the truth about her sister. She's still here."

"How do you know?"

"I've seen her!"

"Where did you see her?"

Hichcock's aggressive tone pushed Cynthia into lying. She replied, "She was in the garden."

Hichcock shook his head, but it was obvious that he was relieved by her response. A slight smile crossed his lips as he said, "The garden, eh? Is she still there? That's rather odd. I doubt Martha would lie."

"Yes, I went out into the garden and I saw her, Bernard."

"Humph ... how odd."

Cynthia threw caution to the wind and asked, "Another thing, Bernard. Where does that door lead to?"

"What door?" The doctor's eyes became hard again.

"The one behind the large mirror."

"Cynthia, you just came out of it so why are you asking me?"

Cynthia for once feeling she had an upper hand, smiled and said, "I saw Martha enter it this afternoon. A hidden room, Bernard?"

"It's my old laboratory. It is not in use now and I would like for it to stay closed, Cynthia."

"Bernard, something has changed since we arrived at Rubens House. Why don't we leave tomorrow and go on holiday in the country to get away from here for a few days? "

Hichcock stiffened and his words came out slow, almost guttural. He said, "I left this . . . house once and I . . . have regretted my actions . . . to this day. Do not ask me to leave Rubens House again . . . Cynthia . . . ever! Good night!"

Hichcock stood for a moment and stared at his wife. His eyes held not the slightest trace of humanity. Rather they were those of a madman. He turned and left the room, leaving his wife distressed and conflicted with emotional turmoil.

CHAPTER ELEVEN

'I pray you let me be at peace,
Get hence, make room for me to die.'
She said that: her poor lip would cease,
Put up to mine, and turn to cry.

I said, 'Bethink yourself how love
Fared in us twain, what either did;
Shall I unclothe my soul thereof?
That I should do this, God forbid.'

A storm was brewing. The fog-shrouded landscape surrounding Rubens House lit up time and again as lightning struck and thunder boomed revealing the dense overgrowth of yard and gardens that had not yet been cleaned up. The ancient house was majestic in its decadent splendor, but the storm brought out the sinister aspect of the house, rather than its beauty, to any who would have passed by on such a night.

Dr. Hichcock lay on his bed fully clothed, his mind holding turmoil of thoughts that would not allow him to sleep. His head turned from side to side and his hands shook visibly as he forced them back into the mattress in an effort to curtail the tremor.

Outside the storm raged. Frustrated, he got up and struck a match to light a candle, but a sound came from below that stilled his hand. He shook the match out and turned his head to the side to better hear what sounded like someone playing the piano in the living room below.

Curious and intrigued, the doctor walked over and opened the door of his room.

Someone was playing the piano. The sound was increasing in intensity as the bridge to Tchaikovsky's Piano Concerto No. 1

reached its climax. It was Margareta's signature piece and the music was as delightful as it was maddening.

Hichcock rushed down the stairs and stopped just above the first floor landing. He peered down into the darkened living room and saw nothing, but the music continued.

The energy from a sudden flash of lightning brought the scene into a momentary state of phosphorescent brilliance.

Hichcock saw a vision of Margareta veiled in white with her eyes closed in rapture as she played the final notes of the Concerto. His body convulsed at the sight and gripped the bannister to keep from falling. A moment later, he burst into the living room, bumping into the grand piano as he slid to a stop.

Another bright flash and crash of thunder and lightning illuminated the room again. No one sat at the piano; only Margareta's big black cat, Jezebel, sat on the bench and hissed at him as Hichhock stared at the scene, his eyes wild in disbelief.

Hichcock turned from the piano to the huge portrait of Margareta that hung beside the stairwell. His body shook involuntarily as if palsied and he began to mutter unintelligible words under his breath.

He turned and ran to the front door, throwing it open; out into the pouring rain he fled. His arms were held up to the sky in supplication as he cried out, "Margareta! My Margareta!"

As if in answer to his plea, the sky sent out a great razor sharp flash of white light that struck the massive front entry gate to the property. Thunder followed a moment later that made the earth tremble beneath his feet.

The cold rain drenched the doctor. In despair, he finally turned and walked, head hung low, back to the open doorway of the house.

Hichcock staggered into the house, leaving behind a trail of water as he fell into one of the living room overstuffed chairs. He was alone. His mind swirled with the vision he had seen of Margareta no more than an hour earlier and he began to cackle to himself, his head rocking back and forth in his trembling hands.

Suddenly, he sat up straight. He leapt from the chair and ran up the stairs. Throwing open the door to his wife's room he burst in and cried out, "Cynthia!"

The room was dark. A flash of lightning revealed the silhouette of a woman in white lace swinging from a noose in front of the open windows. The cold breeze fluttered the curtains drawing them into the room causing the body to swing like a pendulum back and forth. It was drenched with rainwater that ran in rivulets across the polished wooden floor.

The doctor stood in the doorway and stared incredulously at the body's movement until he realized that it had been staged. The figure was that of a mannequin dressed to look like Margareta in her clothing.

Hichcock's mind was now flowing from unreality to reality and back. Realizing that Cynthia was not in the room, he ran down the stairs, gripped with apprehension.

When he got to the first floor, out of breath, he stood with one hand on the piano, bent over to regain his composure. As he looked and wiped cold sweat from his brow, Hichcock spied the silhouette of a woman veiled in white lace crossing the ground beyond the large front window only to disappear into the overgrown gardens beyond.

The doctor ran down the hall and out the still open front door into the pouring rain. He crossed over the same area where he had seen the ghostly figure and yet observed no evidence of footsteps in the muddy ground. He sloshed his way out into the garden, lightning cracking and thunder booming overhead.

"Cynthia! Cynthia!" he cried.

Hichcock walked into a section of uncut gooseberry bushes, their spines ripping and tearing his flesh and clothing as he pulled back the branches to make his way through them.

Just ahead, he saw the white-garbed figure of a woman stumble and fall. Forgetting about the rending the shrubbery was giving him, he tore his way towards the body that lay unmoving in a clearing a few meters away.

When he came upon the figure and looked down, he saw Cynthia in Margareta's white lace dress and white high-ankle boots, now sodden, muddied, and torn.

He looked up only to see the diminutive black clad figure of Martha approaching with umbrella in one hand and an oil lamp in the other. She looked down at the body and said, "She must have fainted."

Hichcock bent over his wife's body and felt her neck for a pulse. "She's alive," he said, "help me get her inside!"

Martha silently obeyed and switched the oil lamp to the hand that held the umbrella and reached down with her free hand to lift under Cynthia's arm while Hichcock did the same with her other arm.

The two hurriedly half-carried, half-dragged the seemingly lifeless body of Cynthia through the slashing rain back into Rubens House.

CHAPTER TWELVE

Yea, though God hateth us, he know
That hardly in a little thing
Love faileth of the work it does
Till it grow ripe for gathering.

Six months, and now my sweet is dead.
A trouble takes me; I know not
If all were done well, all well said,
No word or tender deed forgot.

Hichcock sat straight-backed in a chair in his bedchamber. He faced the painting of Margareta that hung over the fireplace mantle in the room. He had bathed and changed clothing and now wore slacks, slippers, and a burgundy velvet lapelled smoking jacket.

A half-empty bottle of Beefeater gin sat on the floor next to him. Glass in hand, the doctor took a long sip and stared at the painting. Nervously, he got up and unsteadily walked to the window. The reflexion in the glass panes showed one of sordid excitement. His pupils were enlarged and cold sweat beaded the features of the normally aristocratic countenance.

Hichcock picked up the candelabrum and exited the room. There wasn't much night left. His thoughts belonged to the night. There were desires to be fed and, within the house, lay one whose present state could sate his perversions.

The doctor walked next door to Cynthia's room and entered. White sheets pulled back, the unconscious naked body of Cynthia lay across the large Queen Anne bed.

Hichcock lifted the oil lamp high to better illuminate the suppleness of his lovely wife's youthful body. She looked so peaceful in her sleep. Her chest barely moved. It was almost as if she were dead. Setting the lamp beside the bed, he reached down and took her hands, crossing them over her chest in a burial pose.

Upon the touch of her flesh, the doctor shivered, his eyes dilated, and his lips turned downward creating a mask of bestial depravity. His hands began to tremble and he clasped them together, rubbing them in an effort to settle the tremor.

Hichcock continued to look at the body of his wife. His breathing increased and his body continued to shake uncontrollably. He placed his hands close over her body and hesitated before bringing them to his face, then turned and fled from the room.

He reentered his room and walked to the desk, nervously unlocking a drawer to remove a small, ornately carved jewelry box. From the box he extracted a syringe and a vial of brown liquid which he carried back to Cynthia's room. With frantic hands, the doctor held the vial up to the light to check its clarity and then broke it, charging the syringe with the brown liquid.

Cynthia's body lay still upon the bed, still unconscious. Hichcock lifted one of her crossed arms and injected the syringe into her flesh. He placed the vial and syringe in his jacket pocket and then picked up the limp form of his wife and exited the room.

The room was pitch black, emphasized by dozens of candles placed up high and low, illuminating the darkness. Cynthia's nude body lay upon the black mortuary bed. The chill of the room caused her nipples to stand erect and tiny goose bumps were raised on her arms and thighs. She slept a drug-induced slumber and her breathing was so shallow it was almost unnoticed.

A multitude of twinkling lights danced off of the ebony columns that surrounded the bed. In the background, the gramophone played a slightly tinny version of Margareta's version of Beethoven's Piano Sonata No. 32 in C Minor. Hichcock smoothed the black satin sheets around Cynthia's body and, as he did, he leaned close to smell the intoxicating perfume of her flesh.

Outside, the white moon was fading as clouds rolled in to obscure it and a pre-dawn lightness broke over the landscape.
A heavy fog hung low over Rubens House and its environs creating an eerie scene when coupled with the unkempt grounds and the now blackened front entry gate.

The candles were extinguished and tiny tendrils of smoke still drifted upward from a few. Cynthia was waking up. Moving only her eyes, she observed the funeral vestments of the room, the candles, and the ebony columns. From behind a black sheer curtain, a shadow moved towards her. Cynthia's vision was still cloudy from the drug and the light in the room was dim.

The form appeared to be Bernard's, but there was something strange about the way he moved and his features were a bloated rubicund, his face pulsing at the temples and cheeks in a grotesque manner. Cynthia was terrified, but she could not remove her eyes from the repulsive yet fascinating countenance of the man she once loved.

The face came very near. The man's dilated eyes scanned her body once and then came to rest upon her own. They seemed to bore deep into her large brown eyes as if in an effort to see into her psyche. Cynthia was terrified. She held her breath and prayed that the nightmare would end soon.

Suddenly, a thin white hand, deformed and clawed, emerged from the darkness behind her husband to grab his neck. Cynthia screamed and lost consciousness once again.

CHAPTER THIRTEEN

Too sweet, for the least part in her,
To have shed life out by fragments; yet,
Could the close mouth catch breath and stir,
I might see something I forget.

Six months, and I still sit and hold
In two cold palms her two cold feet.
Her hair, half grey half ruined gold,
Thrills me and burns me in kissing it.

Dr. Hichcock walked the long hallway of University Hospital's patient ward accompanied by Dr. Kurt. Hichcock pulled a curtain aside and the men entered a cubicle where Hichcock bent down and put a stethoscope to the chest of a sleeping man.

As he did, Kurt noticed the older physician's neck appeared to have been raked from the throat to the side by a series of four cuts. Curious, he asked, "Professor, what's happened? Your neck ... you're bleeding!"

Hichcock put a hand to his neck, embarrassed, and said, "Ah. .. it was Jezebel, our cat."

Kurt, concerned, said, "Let me at least dress and bandage the wound, Sir!"

"No, there is no need. It is minor and I applied antiseptic myself. I will be fine."

Kurt was about to insist when a nurse's head appeared around the curtain and said, "Professor, the operating room is ready."

Hichcock turned to the nurse and said, "Very well ... prepare the patient for surgery, Nurse. Assemble the interns. Sedate and start a plasma transfusion right away. I will be ready shortly."

Three hours later, Hichcock entered the physician's lounge followed by Dr. Kurt.

Kurt addressed his mentor saying, "Well, that went better than expected. Internal bleeding is always a bit tricky, but you beat the clock, Professor!"

Hichcock was upset and strode to the bar and poured a drink that he downed in one gulp.

"Is something wrong, Sir?"

Hichcock looked at the younger man sideways and said, "You will already know what it is, Edward." Hichcock clasped his hands together to stop the tremor that was coming on him as he sighed, "It's Cynthia!"

"Your wife? But, Professor, how would I—"

Hichcock cut the younger man short and said, "Nonsense, man! You ... know! But what you may not know is that I met her some years back in my travels when she was being treated for a state of shock. I couldn't help falling in love with her right away. She tried to convince me that she was well, but..."

Kurt felt he knew Cynthia and yet he didn't want to unbalance the man who stood before him. He was cautious as he championed her by saying, "Professor, your wife seems to be quite balanced to me. Perhaps she is a bit emotional. But that is her temperament and certainly it is one you can live with."

Hichcock poured another drink without offering one to Kurt. His eyes bored into Kurt and he said, "One I can live with, Edward? Is that not conjecture on your part? Maybe your own feelings for Cynthia influencing your opinion?" Hichcock looked at his hands and back at Kurt. "I do not love Cynthia. I am still in love with my first wife, Margareta. Her ghost is haunting me ...haunting Rubens House!"

Kurt, now angry at the older man's accurate accusation replied, "The blame is yours, Professor!"

Hichcock looked at him in amazement.

"Me?"

"Yes. Your wife, Cynthia, feels like a stranger in your house and why wouldn't she? The fact that you've kept everything as it was when your first wife lived there including all of the portraits of her and even her clothing indicates that you don't love

Cynthia. If you did, you would have removed the memories of your dead wife long ago and shown compassion and love for the wife you have now, Professor!"

Hichcock glared at the younger man and gripped the glass so tight the liquor splashed onto his hand and sleeve.

Kurt continued, "Cynthia is young and vibrant. She needs to feel alive and to be loved! Something you are not giving her..."

"Your accusation is absurd, Edward! What's the harm in bringing Cynthia into my house . . . a place full of wonderful memories for me? It is a fine home and I cannot erase my life for anyone!"

Kurt shook his head and said, "Perhaps it would be enough if you would allow Cynthia to live elsewhere!"

Hichcock contemplated the remark for a moment and then nodded.

"It may be..."

RUBENS HOUSE

The sun was out and the gardens of Mecklenburgh Square were alive with neighborhood families enjoying a break in the weather.

Across from the gardens, the red brick mansion of Rubens House sat forlorn amid tall weeds and an overgrowth of native flora. It was difficult to imagine the yard and gardens as once being the pride of the Square.

It appeared to be abandoned and, as it was a very old home, people associated it with ghosts. As such they avoided going near the property.

Cynthia slept in a chair, her back to the window. A book of Tennyson's poems lay open in her lap. A vase of fresh cut flowers sat on the table beside her.

The windows were open and a light breeze moved the curtains. The sun's rays created cutout patterns in the shadows of the bedchamber.

Dr. Hichcock entered the room. When he saw his wife

sleeping he tried not to make any noise, but Cynthia opened her eyes to see him standing in the doorway. He smiled and said, "How are you, dear? How do you feel?"

Cynthia did not share his levity. Her immediate feelings were of fear. She hesitated before responding to gain control over her emotions. As she did she looked into her husband's eyes that held no conviction to his words.

"What happened to me?"

Hichcock continued to smile and said, "Nothing, my dear. But you are not well. You have good days and bad. Last night you fainted."

He held out the white lace dress that was torn and covered with mud. His lips curled downward and he said in a low voice, "This should be evidence of the state you were in when I found you."

"No, Bernard ... you can not do this—"

"My dear Cynthia, it is just as I suspected and told you. You are experiencing a nervous breakdown. However, try not to worry ... it will pass soon."

Cynthia dropped her head into her hands. What hell life had become since this house ... this physician healer had come into her life. She felt abused and now threatened.

Hichcock looked at his wife for a moment and the smile returned. He turned and left the room without closing the door.

Dr. Hichcock walked down the stairs slowly, deep in thought. When he reached the first floor landing he almost ran into Martha who held a silver tray that contained a glass of milk and a sugar bowl. Master and housekeeper looked at one another in silent understanding. Martha handed the tray to Hichcock who turned without saying a word and retraced his steps back up the stairs.

Dr. Hichcock walked into the bathroom carrying the tray. He looked about him cautiously and then sat the tray on the sink. He opened the medicine cabinet and removed a small, green glass bottle from among many on the shelves. The bottle's label depicted the image of a skull and crossbones and said: POISON

The doctor pulled out a handkerchief, removed the cork from the bottle, and placed the handkerchief tight against its lip, straining its liquid into the glass of milk in an effort to keep sediment from showing in the milk.

He put everything back into place just as if he had never entered the bathroom.

Hichcock returned to Cynthia's bedchamber with the tray that held the glass of milk and the sugar bowl. He smiled at his wife and placed the tray on the table next to the chair where Cynthia still sat powerless, her mind a jumble of emotions. He put two teaspoons of sugar into the milk and lovingly handed the milk to her.

"Here, drink this, dear. It will do you good to take in some nourishment."

Cynthia reluctantly took the glass and sipped the milk.

A sound from the garden attracted Hichcock's attention. He rose up and looked over her to the grounds below. When he looked back down at his wife, she was holding the empty glass in hand and her eyes were flickering as she dozed off.

He smiled and said, "Good! Now you'll have a long sleep, you'll see..."

Cynthia murmured thickly, "Yes, I want to sleep ... let me sleep—" and she closed her eyes.

Hichcock looked at her for a second and then turned and left the room.

CHAPTER FOURTEEN

Love bites and stings me through, to see
Her keen face made of sunken bones.
Her worn-off eyelids madden me,
That were shot through with purple once.

She said, 'Be good with me, I grow
So tired for shame's sake, I shall die
If you say nothing:' even so.
And she is dead now, and shame put by.

Dr. Hichcock walked slowly down the stairs as he had earlier. Again he was lost in thought. When he reached the second floor landing he closed his eyes and leaned against the door to the mortuary room. In a moment of weakness he almost turned to go back upstairs.

When he reopened his eyes, he spied Martha at the bottom of the stairwell on the first floor staring back up at him. Her face was blank, but her eyes bored into his own as if willing him to an end he wasn't sure he wanted.

The doctor walked down to her and the two looked at one another, their eyes implying words that were not spoken. The small black-clad housekeeper held the big black cat, Jezebel, in her arms, stroking him as he purred contentedly.

Hichcock took Jezebel from the old woman's arms and said, "Do not disturb my wife, Martha. She is sleeping. It would be well if you left Rubens House for a few days. You can resume your duties next week."

Martha looked at her employer and seemed to want to say something, but kept her eyes fixed on his and whispered, "As you say, Dr. Hichcock."

Before she could turn to leave, Hichcock added, "I want you

to know I will never forget what you have done for me and my poor wife."

Martha nodded and walked away. The doctor stood thoughtfully stroking the cat and watched the housekeeper as she turned the corner into the dining room.

UNIVERSITY HOSPITAL

A nurse helped Dr. Hichcock into his operating gown and an intern pulled the surgical gloves on his outstretched arms. Dr. Kurt and two interns stood around the operating table that held the figure of a child, a young girl, who cried softly.

Hichcock approached the table. His gloved hands were clasped together as he looked down at the child. His body began to shake and his eyes couldn't see clearly. No, he thought. Not now. The doctor's brow beaded with sweat and those in the room were aware that something was wrong with the Professor.

Suddenly, Hichcock backed away from the table and said quietly, "Dr. Kurt..."

Kurt walked to Hichcock's side of the table and spoke with authority, "Scalpel, nurse..."

An hour later, Hichcock sat in the physician's lounge. Surgical clothing removed, he wore a dark worsted wool suit, slightly disheveled. He sat stiff-backed with a bottle of Beefeater gin on the table in front of him. He was obviously drunk as he sat, glass in hand, and stared blankly at the wall in front of him.

Dr. Kurt walked in and lifted his smock over his head and tossed it in the laundry bin. He looked at the man he considered a mentor and shook his head.

He walked over to Hichcock and picked up the bottle. He tilted it and whistled softly to himself. He looked intently at Hichcock who did not look back.

Finally, he said, "Professor, what is wrong? This..." and he indicated the bottle he held, "... is not who you are! It is not the man I left Vienna to study under!"

Hichcock ignored the younger man.

A moment later, a hospital assistant ran past the lounge doorway and suddenly slid to a stop, sticking his head in the lounge.

"Professor Hichcock...? I'm looking for Professor Hichcock!"

Kurt answered the boy. "You've found him, son. What do you need?"

Relieved, the boy looked at Kurt and said, "Professor Hichcock, there is someone to see you. A Mr. Franz."

Before Kurt could reply, a handsome young man came up behind the boy and said, "Hullo...Bernard!" The man looked beyond Dr. Kurt to Hichcock sitting in the chair.

Hichcock seemed to regain himself and looked up. He spoke slowly so as not to stutter, "Ah, Franz ... You got the bag of clubs?"

Franz walked into the room and said, "No, sir, there was no one in the house!"

Hichcock suddenly focused on the young man and asked in alarm, "No one was at . . . Rubens House?"

"No one. I rang the bell. I knocked on the door. Finally I walked around the house from the outside to see if I could see someone in a window. Nothing! I even tore my pants on some kind of thorn bush. I called out, but no one answered!"

Kurt offered, "Perhaps Mrs. Hichcock was out for a stroll..."

Hichcock, feigning agitation, said, "Dr. Kurt, my wife never goes out alone. I must go and check on her. Franz, I am sorry about the clubs! Something has happened . . . I am sure of it! Kurt, I need to get a coach as soon as possible!" He stood, shakily, and Kurt went to him, concerned, and helped steady the older man on his feet.

Hichcock ran up the stairs in Rubens House. His mind played out the scene he expected to find when he reached Cynthia's room. When he reached her bedchamber, he stood at the door and listened. The house was silent. No sound came from beyond the door. With a satisfied smile, Hichcock opened the door and entered into the room.

Cynthia's bed was empty. He turned to look at the chair. It

was empty, too. Hichcock stood staring dumbfounded at the empty chair. Finally, it dawned on him that the silver tray and the milk glass that Cynthia held when he left her were missing.

He ran to the bathroom to see if the glass was there, but it wasn't. He ran down the stairs towards the kitchen.

CHAPTER FIFTEEN

Yea, and the scorn she had of me
In the old time, doubtless vexed her then.
I never should have kissed her. See
What fools God's anger makes of men!

She might have loved me a little, too,
Had I been humbler for her sake.
But that new shame could make love new
She saw not—yet her shame did make.

The milk glass sat on a table in a laboratory at University Hospital. It was ringed from the milk line to where it had been poured.

Dr. Kurt stood over a brass microscope and peered at a slide under the glass.

Cynthia, elegant in a dark suit, stood beside him, anxious as to his findings. Her voice held an agitated emotion as she said, "The moment that madman took his eyes off me, I poured the milk into a vase of flowers."

Dr. Kurt's voice was calm as he said, "Calm down, Cynthia, if your husband," and he paused for a beat, "if your husband really intended to murder you . . . please, Cynthia, let me finish my analysis before we jump to conclusions."

"Edward, I don't know what to believe any more. My parents are deceased, I have no siblings . . . I have no one . . . other than you that I can count on! You are the only one who can help me!"

Kurt seemed a bit embarrassed as he replied, "Yes, yes of course, Cynthia!"

She clung to his coat sleeve, shaking all over and continued, "The other night I woke up in a horrible place. Bernard looked at me with eyes of a monster, his face pulsating and his hands . . . his hands touched me . . . oh Edward, it was vile, sick..."

"And after that?"

"I don't remember anything else. This morning when I woke up, he was standing there staring at me with that look that seems to see . . . oh, I don't know ... honestly, I don't know what he sees! He left me and then came back with a glass of milk that he'd sweetened with sugar. He told me I needed the nourishment. I pretended to drink it and, as I told you, when he looked away, I poured it out."

"Cynthia, very shortly we will know if the milk was poisoned or not. Once we ... you... know the truth, will you stop the absurdity of your suspicions?"

Cynthia nodded wearily and said, "Is it because he is famous? Is that why he cannot come under any suspicion? What about me, Edward? Why am I the one who you cannot trust?"

Kurt's heart went out to the woman who still held tight to his arm. He did his best to remain calm and said, "Dear Cynthia, I do so want to believe you! We will know shortly."

The sound of footsteps approached the lab and Dr. Kurt and Cynthia looked up to see the silhouette of Dr. Hichcock as he appeared behind the frosted glass of the laboratory door.

Dr. Hichcock opened the door and fixed Cynthia with a look of astonishment.

"Cynthia, I was worried about you. What are you doing here?"

Kurt answered before Cynthia could respond. He said, "Your wife came to look for you, sir. I am afraid I detained her since I knew that you had left the hospital earlier in . . . ah, not the best of circumstances."

Hichcock glared at the younger physician and then turned to his wife and said, "Cynthia, I think it's better that I get you home. If you must, say your goodbyes to Dr. Kurt and let's go."

Throwing a last look of pure venom at Kurt, Hichcock took Cynthia by the arm and pushed her forward toward the door. She offered no resistance.

As they exited the room, Dr. Kurt picked up the glass that

Cynthia had brought him and gazed at it thoughtfully.

The now blackened main entry gate to Ruben House stood open so the coach driver was able to make his way, albeit a tad precariously, up to the front of the old house.

He called, "Whoa, Cassie," and the horse came to a halt. The driver pulled the brake lever and Hichcock opened the carriage door and exited. He held his hand out to Cynthia who refused it.

Hichcock smirked, tossed a coin to the driver who turned the coach, and drove off.

The doctor opened the front door and the couple entered. Cynthia was terrified, but she gathered every ounce of her reserve not to show it to the man with her.

Once inside, Cynthia looked around the quiet house and asked, "Where is Martha?"

"I sent her away."

"What? Have you fired her?"

"Yes. That *is* what you wanted, isn't it? I thought it would make you happy."

Cynthia did not respond. She started up the stairs to her bedchamber.

Hichcock's eyes followed his wife. They were cold and held a calculated determination that Cynthia did not see.

Cynthia entered her room, closing and locking the door. She leaned her back against the door and sobbed within. She heard the sound of a door slamming shut somewhere below.

Soon she heard the sound of heavy footsteps as they trod slowly up the two flights of stairs. Cynthia trembled with fear when the footsteps finally stopped at her door. But a moment later they turned and she heard the sound of her husband's door being opened and closed.

Once her heart had slowed down, Cynthia ran to the wardrobe and opened it, pulling out her suitcase and a few dresses. She then went to the chest of drawers and pulled out a few things, stuffing them into the case.

Tiptoeing softly to the door, Cynthia cracked it to see if the hall landing was clear. It was. She continued to tiptoe and walked to the stairs with her case in hand. By the time she got to the first floor, she was shaking so hard it was difficult for her to stand.

Cynthia looked around and ran for the front door. It was locked. She tried the lock, but it just spun in her fingers. It must have been locked somehow from the outside. She ran through the back of the house and tried a door there. It would not open no matter how hard she pulled.

Cynthia ran back into the living room and pulled the heavy drapes back from the windows. Every window was now barred with wrought iron spikes that prevented entry or . . . exit. As she made her way through the house searching for an escape, the big black cat's eyes followed her and watched everything philosophically as it sat nestled on Margareta's grand piano.

Cynthia, defeated, climbed the stairs back to her room. On the second floor landing she paused. She heard a noise from behind one of the secret doors. She bent down to look through the keyhole of the room she had not been allowed to enter . . . willingly.

What she saw chilled her to the bone. It seemed a thousand candles were burning in a pitch-black room. There was some kind of weird altar surrounded by four columns. In an elevated area, behind the altar, a sheer black curtain silhouetted her husband as he prepared a noose and then tossed it over a ceiling beam to let it swing freely back and forth.

Cynthia felt faint and collapsed against the door, dropping her suitcase which tumbled and fell open, scattering her clothing down the stairwell. A moment later, the mortuary door opened and Cynthia's body was dragged over the threshold of the doorway.

CHAPTER SIXTEEN

I took too much upon my love,
Having for such mean service done
Her beauty and all the ways thereof,
Her face and all the sweet thereon.

Yea, all this while I tended her,
I know the old love held fast his part:
I know the old scorn waxed heavier,
Mixed with sad wonder, in her heart.

A laboratory technician poured a beaker of liquid into the glass that Cynthia Hichcock had dropped off that afternoon. She held the glass up to the overhead gas lighting and swirled it. She then took a syringe, charged it, and placed a few drops on a small square of litmus paper.

This was the same procedure that Dr. Kurt had followed when Cynthia brought the glass in earlier in the day.

The technician viewed the litmus square under the brass microscope. When she rose back up she nodded and said, "Take a look Dr. Kurt. It is, indeed, a powerful anesthetic just as you believed. It would put a horse to sleep!"

"But are you sure?"

"Please, see for yourself."

Kurt walked around the table and looked into the glass. Cynthia was right! Hichcock had either planned to put her to sleep for some reason or he wanted to kill her.

The technician offered, "This is the third time I've tested it with different reagents. Perhaps the one who placed the anesthetic wanted to put someone to sleep, but that sleep would have been eternal if it had been consumed."

Her words make their way into Kurt's mind and reaffirmed his own suspicions. His face took on a look of horror and he called out, "Oh dear God, Cynthia is alone in Rubens House with that madman!"

Dr. Edward Kurt turned and ran from the laboratory.

The ceiling was low and the room seemed to be made of ancient brick and a polished stone. Iron grates were fixed in the walls and darkness lay behind them. A few were open and stone shelves contained coffins that were open and crumbling with mold. Grayish yellow bones were visible in the openings. Also visible were small eyes that occasionally blinked. A skull sat below one of the coffins, lying on its side, covered with cobwebs.

The centerpiece of the oppressive room was a damp concrete slab approximately a meter above the wet limestone floor.

A polished mahogany coffin with ornate silver trim and hinges sat on top of the slab. A name was engraved on a small silver plate on the side of the coffin. It read:

CYNTHIA HICHCOCK 1869 – 1897

The top of the coffin had an oval window at the head end. Behind the oval glass, Cynthia's face was fixed in a paroxysm of fear such as she had never known before. She screamed, but in the padded and sealed coffin, the sound came out muffled and indistinct.

Cynthia tore at the padded lining in an attempt to reach the rivets of the hinges, but her nails broke and her fingers bled. The oval glass soon steamed up and her face was no longer in view. She tried to scream again, but only silence came forth, ending in a violent fit of coughing and sucking in air to breath.

Cynthia pushed up with her knees and hands, but the lid was sealed so tight that it didn't budge with her efforts.

In a last throe of despair, Cynthia attempted to turn first to one side and then the other, but there wasn't enough space in the coffin for her to turn completely sideways. Finally, she thought to rock herself from side to side as hard and fast as she could.

It worked! Cynthia felt the coffin move a few inches. She rocked again with the intensity of a raging animal. The coffin continued to move and finally it teetered on the concrete slab and then it fell, landing on its side and falling back on its base. The front locking hinges snapped and the front side and lid popped free of the deathtrap.

Cynthia rolled out of the broken coffin and dragged herself across the wet floor. She bled from a shoulder wound and her fingers left steaks of red where she clawed her way across the mold-covered floor. She passed the cobweb-laden skull and it moved, causing her to whimper as she tried to edge away. A pinkish tail showed beside it and quickly disappeared.

Cynthia lost track of time. Eventually she found herself in front of the iron gate that led into the tunnels under Rubens House. The gate was closed and, when she reached up and pushed, it did not move.

As Cynthia lay there helpless, looking at the gate that offered her a way out of the crypt, she saw a vision she had seen before.

A pair of high collar white lace-up boots and the hem of a white lace dress led Cynthia's eyes up a ghostly figure that ended with a white veil that covered the figure's face.

Cynthia's mind was so clouded with pain and fear that she was not sure if she was hallucinating or not. The face behind the veil looked like that of Margareta in the paintings, except it was now ancient with gray hair, wild eyes, and a disfiguring scar that ran down one eye and cheek.

The woman looked down at Cynthia and intoned hoarsely, "You will not escape! I'll bury you alive as they buried me..."

Cynthia let out a bloodcurdling scream and, summoning strength she didn't know she had, rose up and pushed the gate open. She bumped into the ghost of Margareta and ran down the tunnel in terror.

The chase was on. Margareta ran after Cynthia unhinged, laughing hysterically, taunting the young woman with the horrors that lay in store for her.

"You cannot run away, child! You were not scarred as I was when you got free of the coffin! I need your skin . . . I need . . . your blood ... and I will soon have them!"

Cynthia ran through her pain. She ran through her fear. She ran unseeing in a world that her adversary knew much better than she did.

The mad cackling laughter of the insane Margareta followed her as she made her way through the labyrinth of dirt and stone.

CHAPTER SEVENTEEN

It may be all my love went wrong—
A scribe's work writ awry and blurred,
Scrawled after the blind evensong—
Spoilt music with no perfect word.

But surely I would fain have done
All things the best I could. Perchance
Because I failed, came short of one,
She kept at heart that other man's.

Cynthia ran until her feet landed on wood. She stopped, immediately remembering the last time she was lost in the tunnel. That horrible night, she followed the light to an underground room, the room where Martha served tea. Her feet were on solid wood just before the door that evening and that was the only wooden floor she had felt in the tunnel. Maybe, just maybe, she was near the same door.

Cynthia held her arms out before her and felt along the tunnel wall. The dirt turned to stone and brick and within a few minutes she had victory! A door! She had found a door!

Cynthia tried the knob and the door opened. Miraculously, it was the same room and it was empty. A candelabrum sat on a table and it held a single lit candle so she could see again. She remembered that when Martha entered the room with the silver tray she had entered from another door.

Cynthia didn't hesitate. She picked up the candelabrum and went straight for the door. Beyond it was a narrow set of stairs that led upward. She had no idea where the stairs led but she did not have time to waste.

Cynthia attacked the stairs, driven by fear. When she came to a door at the top she threw herself at it and burst into a strange, candle-lit room. In front of her hung a swinging rope noose. It had to be the one she had spied Bernard make the other evening. That meant that she was in the . . . death room!

Cynthia thought at least she was above ground in the house. She spotted the door that led into the second floor landing and determined to make her way to it. She parted the sheer black curtains and stepped down from the elevated area, quickly walking past lit candles of every shape and size surrounding the weird altar that was, in reality, some kind of bed.

"Nooooo!" she cried as she attempted to open the door. It was locked.

Cynthia stood at the door and turned to face the room. She had been through hell and pure adrenalin kept her upright. She bled from the shoulder wound and her fingers throbbed with each heartbeat.

A loud scratching noise sounded and then a piano played. But it was different piano. The sound was slightly off, a tinny sound. The song was familiar. It was Beethoven's Piano Sonata No. 32 in C Minor. Cynthia was unable to pinpoint the source of the music. It seemed to come from everywhere as it echoed eerily throughout the weird room.

As the music played, a singsong cackling laughter rang through the room. Cynthia saw a black velvet curtain part to one side of the bed. The ghost of Margareta stood with the big black cat, Jezebel, in her arms. Both sets of eyes were locked on Cynthia. The cat hissed when Cynthia's back hit the door.

The ghost or woman, Cynthia wasn't sure, stared at her; the eyes held insanity and the mouth either sneered or grinned hysterically. A long livid scar ran over one eye and along the cheek.

Cynthia was trapped and sometimes when an animal is trapped it will attack. Within Cynthia, an animalistic rage that had been building suddenly exploded and, in a fury, she ran at the woman, her bloody clawed hands ready to tear and rend.

Margareta did not move. She laughed hysterically and called out, "Come to me, child . . . I need your skin! I need your blood!"

Just before Cynthia's hands could close around Margareta's neck, two hands grabbed her from behind and closed in on her throat.

Dr. Bernard Hichcock stood behind her, his face no longer human as he squeezed his fingers tightly around the throat of his wife. His eyes were enlarged, his temples and cheeks pulsed, and his mouth twitched as he gibbered, "Margareta, Margareta, my Margareta..."

Dr. Edward Kurt's boots pounded the gravel drive that led up to Rubens House. He threw himself against the entrance door, but it was locked. His efforts at shoving and hammering on the massive wooden door were futile. It wouldn't give. Kurt stepped back and looked at the ancient house. The windows were barred and Kurt now realized that it wasn't to keep intruders out, but to hold Cynthia captive. He must save her!

A woman's blood curdling scream echoed somewhere overhead. Kurt was frantic, but it was imperative that he kept his head or he would have no chance to save the woman he loved.

He ran to and took hold of one of the ornamental railings that ran along the sides of the main entry door. He placed a boot into a rung and climbed until he found himself standing flush to the wall on an intricate iron motif of a lion's head just above the main door. He stretched as far as he dared and reached out to the lower ironwork of one of the second floor terraces.

The stretch was too far. His fingers just brushed the lower bar of the terrace. He would have to jump for it.

Kurt had no way to gain momentum. It was a make it or fail scenario. With clarity, Cynthia's words came back to him. She said, "I have no one . . . other than you that I can count on! You are the only one who can help me!"

He would have to make it or she would be dead before morning!

The scream sounded again and it ended in a prolonged sob. Kurt leapt and his right hand caught hold of the iron bar. His body swung like a pendulum until he could reach his left hand up and grasp the bar. He pulled himself hand over hand up the geometric pattern of the iron railing and finally threw a leg over the rail to stand on the terrace.

Immediately, Kurt went to work on the window. It was locked shut so he placed the tail of his coat against the glass and hit it hard with a balled fist, shattering it. Using his coat, Kurt knocked the loose glass out of the frame. He reached in and unclasped the lock. Kurt pushed the window open and jumped inside. He stood for just a moment to orient himself with his location in the house.

A muffled inhuman sounding laughter came from somewhere just ahead of him. Kurt ran blindly, seeking the source of the sound.

Cynthia hung upside down; her feet held fast in the tight noose that Hichcock had fastened to the ceiling beam above. Her arms were strapped to her sides with a leather belt and she swung slowly from side to side. A low moan escaped her lips and her eyes were as large as saucers as she watched the scene that unfolded in front of her.

The dark room was illuminated with hundreds of candles of all shapes and sizes. It was cold. The gramophone played the same sonata again and again and the strange music added to the unreality of what was happening.

Dr. Hichcock stood with a gleaming silver scalpel in his hand. He held it up and the hand shook as if palsied. Hichcock grimaced and grasped his scalpel hand with his free hand.

"Stop . . . not now!" he said and took a deep breath. He let go and the hand stilled. A slack jawed grin erupted on his face and he said to himself, "Yes, yes . . . I'm ready for surgery now..."

As Cynthia watched, she knew that her husband, Bernard Hichcock, had finally lost all touch with reality.

Margareta, arrayed in a badly soiled white lace dress, stood behind a sheer black curtain and tittered to herself.

Hichcock spoke to his first wife. "Margareta! Everything will be as before, my love . . . I will restore your beauty ... look at that skin, Margareta ..."

As he spoke, he reached out and touched Cynthia's face and the cold of the scalpel brushed her cheek. Cynthia screamed until nothing but a gargling sound came forth from her lips.

From behind the curtain, Margareta's voice cackled, "Yes Bernard, kill her!" Her tittering continued as the piano played endlessly in the background.

CHAPTER EIGHTEEN

I am grown blind with all these things:
It may be now she hath in sight
Some better knowledge; still there clings
The old question. Will not God do right?

Evening fell and Rubens House was clothed in darkness. It was pitch black inside the hallway. Dr. Edward Kurt ran blindly in the darkness. Suddenly, he stumbled and pitched forward hitting a wall, then fell backward upon the carpeted floor. He rolled over and slammed his fists into the carpet, cursing himself for such foolishness.

Knowing darkness was falling, in his haste to get to Cynthia, Kurt had neglected to bring a torch. When he got inside the window and heard the scream, it was too late to locate a lamp. All he thought to do was run in an effort to find and save the woman he had grown to love. But his foolishness had cost him precious time and, for all he knew, Cynthia could be dead at the hands of her husband, the insane Dr. Hichcock.

As Kurt was getting to his feet, another scream sounded. She is alive! Cynthia is still alive. He listened intently to determine what direction the screaming was coming from. It took all the self-restraint that was within him not to run blindly again.

Kurt took out his matches and located a lamp that stood on a nearby hall table. He lit it and turned the wick down low. The yellow glow threw a weird, distorted likeness of his visage upon the high walls. He moved forward and back down the direction that he had come from. He would find her; he MUST find her before it was too late.

Dr. Hichcock's hand trembled ever so slightly as he brought the gleaming scalpel to Cynthia's throat. She struggled in her bonds and then froze as the horror of the blade got close to her skin.

Margareta's voice sounded old and feeble as she cackled, "Give me her blood ... I need her blood!"

Dr. Hichcock looked over at his first wife and then back down at his second. A moment of self-pity washed over him and he attempted to still his hand with anticipation of what was to come. He held Cynthia's leg with one hand to keep her from rocking and with his other hand he brought the knife blade to her throat. A tiny pinpoint of blood showed where it touched her delicate skin. He stood mesmerized staring at the drop of blood that grew larger and then trailed down the lovely white neck. It was such a shame, thought Hichcock, but the sound of Margareta's voice brought him back to reality as she urged him to finish his task.

"Do it, Bernard! Finish her so that I may live again!"

Suddenly, before his blade could continue its arc across her neck, the door burst in with a loud crash. Dr. Kurt shouldered his way into the room like a bull charging a matador de toros.

"Stop! Stop it this instant, you fool!"

Hichcock slowly withdrew the blade from Cynthia's throat. His glazed eyes refocused and a snarl emanated from his wet lips. The older man looked at the younger who was untying Cynthia's bound arms. Hichcock threw himself against Kurt and attempted to bring the blade against some portion of Kurt's anatomy.

Dr. Hichcock was amazingly strong for a man of his age or perhaps it was his insanity that fueled him into a sort of superhuman strength. Kurt had to fight with all of his cunning and reserve for his life and for Cynthia's.

The fight was brutal. The blade did, indeed, do its work, drawing blood multiple times along Kurt's arms and from a long thin cut running down his right cheekbone. But the younger man had the advantage of stamina that came with his youth and, finally, Kurt was able to best Hichcock, knocking his hand against a wall and causing Hichcock to drop the scalpel.

Kurt held back no mercy as he slammed his fist into Hichcock's face time and again. He grabbed the madman by his shirt collar and flung him backwards into a row of lit candles knocking them over. One of the candles tipped over into a velvet drapery and suddenly the funeral vestments of the room were violently ablaze as if they had been doused in petrol.

Taking no thought for his own injuries, Kurt ran back to free Cynthia, but the ancient hag, Margareta, stood between him and the girl, wearing a soiled white lace dress. It was the same one she had worn so resplendently in the painting somewhere downstairs.

The old woman tittered and her eyes rolled up into her head as she shouted in a hoarse voice, "Noooo, you can't have her! She is mine. Mine! I will live because of her!" With those words, Margareta raised her clawed hands and charged Kurt, raking his face with broken nails that drew uneven lines of scarlet from his forehead to his cheeks.

By now his face was a mask of red and his vision was blurry from smoke and blood. Kurt grabbed the crone by her neck and shoved her out of the way in his effort to get back to Cynthia who was now swinging perilously close to the burning drapes. Margareta fell into the funeral vestments and her dress caught fire. She screamed a hideous sound and then laughed manically as the flames engulfed her. The sound reverberated in the small room as it counted the never-ending sonata that still played on the gramophone in the background.

Hichcock rose up as if from the dead and ran to Margareta's side. He tried to stop the fire from climbing Margareta's dress by wrapping her with his coat, but the flames spread from her to him, turning both the physician and his reanimated wife into human torches.

The fire was transforming the mortuary room into a funeral pyre. Kurt lifted Cynthia free from the hook and unbound her feet. He picked her up in his arms and she clung to him with her head buried in his chest. Just before they fled the room, both young people looked back to see the flaming Dr. Hichcock place his arms in a death embrace around the now charred non-recognizable remains of Margareta. A horrible wailing sound issued forth from his throat just before both figures crumpled to the floor, two grotesquely disfigured lifeless forms emitting the stench of smoldering flesh.

The front door of the once beautiful red brick mansion called Rubens House burst open and a dense gray smoke rushed out into the cool night air. Kurt, coughing, bloody, and singed from head to booted toe, exited the main entrance with Cynthia in his arms. He half stumbled and half ran down the steps and through the garden and out to the massive arched entryway. Behind them, Rubens House was engulfed in flames that rose high into the night sky. The couple could hear amid the cracking of timbers the clanging of an approaching fire truck and the murmur of the Mecklenburgh Square neighbors that came to stare at the horrible yet fascinating sight of the burning landmark.

Cynthia raised her face from Kurt's chest and turned to look at the house of horrors with eyes full of terror. Kurt gently took her chin and turned her head and eyes back towards him.

Cynthia's eyes softened and tears streamed down her face. She said, "Darling, you saved my life …"

Kurt, his voice husky with emotion, tried to sound cheerful as he said back to her, "Come on, my dear! You're safe now. The nightmare is over. Let's get away from this place."

Cynthia smiled and laid her head back on Kurt's chest, clutching his neck tightly. He gazed lovingly upon her as he carried her off the estate and away from the horrible Dr. Bernard Hichcock into the beginning of a brighter future.

FINE

Michael Hudson is the mastermind behind two boutique publishing ventures, Sequential Pulp Comics and Raven's Head Press.

He has licensed and worked with King Features, Inc., Condé Nast, C3 Entertainment, Dark Horse Comics, Random House, Edgar Rice Burroughs, Inc., and Frank Frazetta just to name a select few.

His desire has always been to create and publish. He is an accomplished painter and illustrator and has been writing for many years. Michael is the author of four novels all published by Raven's Head Press.

He currently resides in Clearwater, Florida where he continues to write and publish works of fiction that interest him.

Ernesto Gastaldi (Born September 10, 1934) is an Italian author, screenwriter, and director. He has published a dozen books, mostly thriller, science fiction and humor. He is one of the few Italian authors to be published under his own name in an American magazine, *The Magazine of Fantasy and Science Fiction* in 1965, with his story *The End of Eternity* (translated into English by Harry Harrison.)

He has written more than 100 films, starring some of the greatest actors in the world including Sophia Loren, Marcello Mastroianni, Henry Fonda, Anthony Quinn, Telly Savalas, Carroll Baker, Barbara Steele, Terence Hill, Budd Spencer, Jack Palance, James Mason, Steve McQueen, Van Johnson, Daliah Lahvi, Pamela Tiffin, Lee VanCleef, Jean-Louis Trintignant, James Coburn, Mel Ferrer, Glenn Ford, Giancarlo Giannini, Robert DeNiro and many others.

His scripts have been directed and produced by well-known directors such as Sergio Leone, Tonino Valerii, Mario Bava, Riccardo Freda, Mario Camerini, Lucio Fulci, Damiano Damiani, and Sergio Leone among many others. Gastaldi ahs also directed six films including one of the fist and greatest giallo films of all time, Libido in 1965 starring his wife, Mara Maryl.

During that period he became one of the most important and prolific writers of peplum, giallo, spaghetti western and horror films. Among the best-known titles The Whip and the Body, Days of Wrath, My Name is Nobody, The Grand Duel, The Case of the Bloody Iris, and Once Upon a Time in America. Many of his western and giallo films have achieved a cult status around the world.

Since 1955 he's lived in Rome, where he married the actress Mara Maryl. He is the father of three children, born in 1961, 1966, and 1974.

ore Exciting Pulp Adventure
From Raven's Head Press

THE STARKENDEN QUEST

by Gilbert Collins
Cover painting by Lawrence Sterne Stevens • Interior illustrations by Virgil Finlay

Down on his luck and down to his last few shillings, John Crayton finds himself marooned in Yokohama at the Four Winds Hotel. A financial disaster has nearly wiped out his bank account back home in England and he needs a job quickly in order to pay his hotel bill or risk jail in Japan. He and a similarly unemployed friend have a fortuitous encounter with the shady and morose Abel Starkenden in a local bar that changes their luck.

The Starkenden Quest has overtones of Haggard, Bedford-Jones and all the Indiana Jones movies. Starkenden and his two explorers-for-hire encounter a run-in with Chinese pirates, crossing a raging river of white rapids in a most unusual fashion, and travelling through an ancient cavern equipped with a lantern made from a human skull.

Collins is well worth investigating for readers who like intelligent rousing adventures. First published in 1925 by Gerald Duckworth and Co. *The Starkenden Quest* was popular enough in its day to merit an abridged version in the pulp magazine *Famous Fantastic Mysteries* in the October 1949 issue. The Raven's Head Press edition contains a foreword by genre fiction critic J.F. Norris who gives us a fascinating insight into the man behind the novel, Gilbert Collins.

A ROUSING ADVENTURE NOVEL IN THE LOST RACE GENRE WITH DWARFISH APE-LIKE CREATURES, A HIDDEN TREASURE TROVE OF GEMS, A MUMMY, A WHITE GODDESS, A LOVE INTEREST AND HEROIC CHARACTERS FIGHTING FOR THEIR LIVES. THIS IS PULP...RAVEN'S HEAD PRESS edition $19.95 US • Order your copy today from Amazon.com or Ravensheadpress.com

MORE EXCITING PULP NOIR FROM RAVEN'S HEAD PRESS

Ramona Stewart's
DESERT TOWN

A HOTHOUSE MELODRAMA

DESERT TOWN is dark crime fiction for those who have a taste for the perverse and violent. It was made into a major film, DESERT FURY, starring Burt Lancaster, Lizbeth Scott and Mary Astor.

It's the story of seventeen year old Paula Haller as she transitions into womanhood while defying her mother, Fritzi's dominance. Fritzi runs the small town of Chuckawalla including the Purple Sage casino and saloon as well as a bordello or two. Fritzi can control everything but Paula and the tension between the two is drawn as tight as a drum.

The scenery includes sprawling ranches, a very much out of place colonial mansion and the beauty of the vast desert.

Mix in a notorious gangster, his insanely jealous business associate, a love triangle, some sadistic cops, weirdly eccentric characters and sexual innuendo aplenty.

Once the sun brings all these ingredients to a boil you've got the recipe for a crackerjack noir story like no other.

RAVEN'S HEAD PRESS edition $14.99 US • Order your copy today from Amazon.com or ravensheadpress.com

Printed in Great Britain
by Amazon